BARTHOLOMEW

EMPIRE
BOOK 1

PENELOPE SKY

HARTWICK PUBLISHING

Hartwick Publishing

Bartholomew

Copyright © 2023 by Penelope Sky

All rights reserved.

No part of this book may be reproduced in any form or by any electronic or mechanical means, including information storage and retrieval systems, without written permission from the author, except for the use of brief quotations in a book review.

CONTENTS

1.	Bartholomew	1
2.	Bartholomew	7
3.	Bartholomew	21
4.	Bartholomew	47
5.	Laura	51
6.	Bartholomew	65
7.	Laura	71
8.	Bartholomew	85
9.	Laura	107
10.	Bartholomew	137
11.	Laura	155
12.	Bartholomew	173
13.	Laura	179
14.	Bartholomew	209
15.	Laura	217
16.	Bartholomew	231
17.	Laura	241
18.	Bartholomew	263
19.	Laura	287
20.	Laura	325
21.	Bartholomew	341
22.	Laura	355
23.	Bartholomew	365

1

BARTHOLOMEW

The days grew longer. The nights shorter.

Gray clouds were replaced by sunshine, and rainy afternoons were replaced by colorful flowers. Paris came alive once again, the lights from the Eiffel Tower shining like a star rather than a lighthouse in the fog.

I hated it.

I sat alone at the bar. It emptied out shortly after I arrived, either because people didn't like the look of me, or because it was almost midnight on a Tuesday. My half-full glass was my company, along with the bartender, who cast worried glances my way. I was the only reason he had to keep this place open, but he wouldn't dare ask me to leave.

Finally, my guest arrived.

He stepped out of the cold and into the bar, in a long-sleeved shirt and dark jeans. His bright eyes found mine, and with a subtle look of annoyance, he joined me at the bar.

I rapped my knuckles against the counter. "Another for my friend here."

The bartender was quick to help us, sliding the glass across the counter.

I held up my glass to him. "To old friends."

Benton held my gaze for a second before he clinked his glass against mine. "And old enemies."

The corner of my mouth lifted with a smile, and I drank.

He did the same.

We hadn't spoken in six months, but his life had changed substantially. He was married now and had just found out he had a baby on the way.

I'd congratulate him, but it sounded like a miserable existence to me. "My invitation must have gotten lost in the mail."

"It was just the three of us."

"Did you knock her up on purpose, or...?"

"Yes." Benton flashed his fierce eyes on me. "There are people out there who think children are a blessing rather than a curse."

"I'm definitely not one of those people."

"You don't say." He took a drink. "How are things in the Catacombs?"

"Stale."

"Are we talking about the air quality or business?"

"Both." I brought the glass to my lips and took a drink.

"I find it hard to believe business has been stagnant with Roan out of the picture."

I turned to him, my eyebrow slightly raised. "How did you know that?"

"Bleu."

I was certain Benton disapproved of his brother's choice, but he didn't ask me to fire him. "Croatia isn't that big of a market."

"You're still moving millions of pounds a week."

"I hear the Skull King does more."

Benton went rigid when he heard what I'd said. "I'd hoped you moved on from that."

"Looks like you don't know me as well as I thought."

"You have more than enough, Bartholomew."

"Until I have everything, it'll never be enough."

Benton studied me, his blue eyes showing all his thoughts like words on a page. "I understand the high you get with every conquest. It fades...and then you need another. With every bullet that misses your heart, with every skull you smash beneath your boot, it gives you something you can't find anywhere else. But it'll never fix the problem, Bartholomew. It'll never fill that hole."

"What hole?" I asked, my lips slightly curled in amusement.

Benton stared at me, refusing to actually say it.

I swirled the glass, watching the liquor spin like water in a flushed toilet. "The Skull King's days are limited."

"And then what happens when he's dead? There'll just be another."

I tipped my head back and took a drink before I tapped the glass to the counter. "Not if I take his place."

2

BARTHOLOMEW

France shared a border with Italy, but the distance between us was still infinite. To control a territory that far away required intense delegation and management. I was up for the job and ready to kill anyone who resisted.

But I needed to know my enemy—and that required research.

It required spies.

It required massive payoffs.

I stepped into the living room, barefoot and bare-chested, wearing sweatpants with nothing underneath because I'd just finished with my favorite whore in the bedroom. Bleu was there waiting for me, a pitcher of ice water and a glass placed there by my butler. A black folder was sitting there as well.

I took a seat in the armchair, knees spread wide apart, sweat still on my back that smeared against the leather chair.

Bleu didn't look directly at me, as if he wanted to respect my privacy by ignoring the sex written all over me.

I grabbed a cigar from the bowl and lit it, the smoke rising straight to the ceiling. I sank into the armchair with my elbow on the armrest. "You came here for a reason?"

He grabbed a cigar for himself, probably to cover the stench I brought into the room. "Very little intel I was able to gather. His crew is pretty tight."

"But every man has a weakness. Wife. Kid. Deadly allergy…something."

"No wife. And he has no medical records, which tells me his ties to the underworld precede his birth."

So this guy was the real deal.

"But."

"Ooh…I like the sound of that."

"He has a couple daughters."

"This just got interesting." I rested my arm, the smoke rising to the ceiling and making my living room smell like an old chimney.

"One is with him. One he's been estranged from for seven years. They haven't spoken once."

Now my interest was really piqued. "That sounds promising."

"I'm not sure if she'll be much use to us. If they don't speak, can we really use her as leverage?"

"Depends on why they stopped speaking."

Bleu answered the unspoken question. "No idea. I only came across her existence by accident. He really scrubbed her from his life, like he doesn't want anyone to know she exists."

I puffed another cloud of smoke from my mouth. "Where is she now?"

He handed the black folder to me. "In Paris, actually."

"You don't say..." I opened the folder and found a large photo. It was a young woman with deep brown hair, skin that looked like olive oil. I could taste it on my tongue as

I stared. Her eyes were the color of espresso with a dollop of cream in the center. Plump lips like clouds, painted a muted pink.

"She's a personal shopper. Has a lot of high-end clients."

"As in, she shops for people?"

"Yes."

I flipped the page and found another picture. It was a full-body photo, her stepping out of a café with a coffee in hand. She wore a long-sleeved dress with knee-high boots, a purse dangling in the crook of her elbow. I didn't say this a lot, but I said it now. "Damn."

"She has an office in the city."

I flipped through more pictures, growing more impressed with every image. "I'll have to stop by."

"Should I get the team together?" he asked. "We can grab her when she leaves her office."

"There's a chance she's being watched. Italian men don't usually abandon their family. Not truly, anyway." I closed the folder. "I'll stop by. See what I find."

I sat in my car across the street.

Her small office was wedged between a clothing store and a café. Through the front window, I could see men's and women's shoes on display, along with handbags and wallets. There was clothing too. Jackets, because it was still a little chilly outside, but also some lighter stuff because of the approaching warm months.

I sat there for two hours, and from what I could tell, no one kept tabs on her.

She was entirely on her own.

I crossed the street and looked through the glass before I walked inside.

She stood at the counter, the phone pressed to her ear while she scribbled notes on a notepad. She was in a sweater that only covered one shoulder, and her hair was in loose curls over her exposed skin. When I stepped inside, a quiet bell rang overhead, and she continued to talk like she didn't realize I was there.

"Got it." She continued her notes. "Cynthia. Cynthia, just listen to me, alright?" she said with a note of humor in her voice. "How long have you been coming to me? A *long* time, right? Because you know I know what I'm doing. I know how to make a man beg. And trust me, that piece-of-shit ex-husband of yours is going to swallow his tongue when he sees you. Come in next Tuesday, and I'll show you what I got. Bye, girl." She hung up the phone, finished her notes, and then looked up at me.

Her vibrant mood faded once her eyes settled on me. She was like a deer caught in the headlights, unsure what to do at the sight of me. Something about my appearance clearly unnerved her. I was in my leather jacket and boots, so I didn't exactly belong there with her designer dresses and purses.

She came around the counter and approached me, sizing me up like she was taking my measurements in her head. "Let me guess. Your wife threw you out, and this is all you have." She wore light-colored jeans and pumps, smelling like a rose garden. She looked me up and down, her arms crossed over her chest.

"I'm not married."

"Anymore, or...?"

Her eyes were like magnets. I couldn't stop staring at them. They had a smoky look to them, her lashes thick and dark, perfectly complementing the natural color of her eyes. There was more to it than that, but I couldn't put my finger on it. "Never been married."

"So…what's with the outfit?"

I walked into a lot of serious situations, but I'd never been thrown off my game like this. My eyebrows dropped over my eyes. I could feel just how confused I looked. "What's wrong with it?"

"Well, it's broad daylight, and you look like you're about to head to the club. That's why I asked if you were married. Maybe you were out late last night and came home to all your stuff burned in the fireplace. Not the first time it's happened…" She looked me up and down again, her arms still squeezing her narrow waist. "I get that sort of thing a lot. No one appreciates a woman more than a newly divorced man who realizes how much she did for him only when she's gone. Doesn't even know how to pick out his own clothes."

It was hard not to stare at her face. Those eyes. That confidence. The front of her sweater was slightly tucked into her jeans so I could see her hips. Womanly hips. No one had ever spoken to me like this, but I imagined if she knew who I was, she would *still* speak to me like this.

I was fucking intrigued.

"Let me take your measurements. We'll go from there." She turned around and headed to the counter to get her measuring tape.

Maybe it was just the jeans, but this woman had an ass I'd never forget.

She returned to me and started with my arm, measuring the length from my shoulder to wrist. Then she checked the thickness by wrapping the tape around my biceps. She checked my shoulders, my back, the length of my torso.

Then she moved to her knees.

Right in front of me.

She wrapped the tape around one of my thighs.

I stared down at her, imagining her tugging down my jeans as fast as she could so she could eat my dick.

She measured my inseam. My outseam. My jeans were suddenly a little snugger. I was sure she noticed—and I hoped she did.

And then she was back on her feet again. "What line of work are you in?" Her hair fell back slightly when she straightened. Her shoulders were poised, her stomach tight, her spine straight.

I got lost in her features as I tried to think of an answer. Well, an appropriate one, at least. I was a straightforward guy, telling people the truth with blunt trauma. "Pharmaceutical sales."

"So, you'll need a couple dress shirts and slacks for work, and then some casual outfits. You know, so you don't look like the Terminator." Her lips tugged up in a smile, and her eyes brightened just a bit.

I think she was teasing me.

She returned to her place behind the calendar and made some notes. "I think I can have everything to you within a week. I offer free delivery, so I can drop it off at your place." She looked at me, her eyes expectant.

Let the enemy see where I live? Sure, why not? "That would be convenient."

She grabbed a pen and wrote down my address. "Thank you for your business. I have all clothing tailored to your specifications, so you're going to love everything I pick out for you."

I'd throw that shit in the closet and never look at it again. "Your name?"

"Laura. Yours?"

"Bartholomew."

"Wow, that is a very unusual name."

"I'll see you next week, Laura." I walked out of the shop and onto the sidewalk, my movements slightly hindered by the enormous rod in my pants.

A week had come and gone, and I sat on the couch in my living room in just my sweatpants, waiting for my guest to arrive with the stupid clothes I would never wear. I'd never worn slacks in my life. Even at black-tie events, I wore whatever the fuck I wanted. And if I ever touched a collared shirt, it was because I was strangling someone with it.

One of my men entered the room. "She's arrived, sir."

I gave him a nod in dismissal. The news was on the TV. Tonight's story was about a shooting that took place in a bad neighborhood. Cocaine was sprinkled in the street, like bullets had pierced the bricks. Police were on the scene, they would book everything into evidence, but of course, it would never lead anywhere. There were no witnesses either—because I killed all of them. Imbeciles thought they could sell my product at a higher price and start their own business.

Bitch, please.

I turned off the TV.

Heels echoed from the other side of the floor, so I knew Laura and my butler had stepped off the elevator.

A moment later, they emerged, Laura carrying several outfits on hangers with a protective covering. "Special delivery." Her voice was as perky as those tits.

I rose to my feet and approached her, studying her reaction to my bare chest.

Her eyes remained focused on me, as if in defiance.

A stretch of silence passed between us.

I finally took the clothes out of her hands. "Thank you."

My butler immediately took them and carried them to my bedroom.

"How much do I owe you?"

"You don't want to try them on first?"

Why? I was just going to drop them off at a donation center. "I trust you." I grabbed the checkbook off the table, wrote down the total with a generous tip, and handed it to her.

She didn't check the amount before she pocketed it. "Thank you, Bartholomew."

I liked the way she said my name, pronouncing every syllable like she was trying to memorize it and get it right.

I could help her with that in my bedroom right now.

"You know where to find me."

She stared.

I stared.

I wasn't sure what I expected to happen. I wanted her in my bedroom, her luscious thighs squeezing my hips, her ankles locked right at the top of my ass, her nails buried deep in my back as she said my name over and over again…

But I didn't know how to make that happen.

She wasn't a whore, so I couldn't pay her.

And she was my enemy, so that was a bit complicated.

Bleu appeared from another room. "Bartholomew." He didn't say anything more in front of Laura and walked away.

She glanced at him then turned back to me. "Good night." She turned around and returned the way she came, her nectarine ass snug in her jeans, especially with those pumps.

I stared down the hallway until I heard the light hum of the elevator.

She was gone.

I stepped into the parlor where Bleu waited for me. "Rick just called. They've got a situation over at the docks."

"What kind of situation?" I asked calmly, still thinking about pussy.

"The cops are patrolling the dock, and we have a delivery tonight."

I released a sigh. "The cops don't usually interfere unless we make it public."

"I guess they have a new chief. Really strict on crime, especially drugs. Apparently, his son died from an overdose."

I rolled my eyes. "Only idiots die from overdoses, and if he doesn't want to join his son, he better back off. I don't like to kill cops, but I'll slaughter each and every one of them if they make me."

"I know."

I paced the parlor, thinking about work and not about pussy. "Tell Rick to change ports. We'll work out the rest."

"Got it," Bleu said. "And what about the girl? Now would be a good time to grab her."

She'd walked right into my lair without protection. Didn't even have to snatch her off the street or sneak into her apartment and drug her. I could keep her as a prisoner until I was ready to use her.

But I didn't do any of those things.

"Let her go," I said. "I want to have some fun with her first."

3

BARTHOLOMEW

A few days later, I returned to her small store.

Like last time, she was on the phone. "I knew you'd like that blazer. The padding in the shoulders is discreet but gets the job done. I'll grab you a few more in other colors. Thanks, Brian." She hung up then lifted her chin to look at me.

No playfulness. No brightness in her eyes. In fact, she looked displeased to see me. "Was there something wrong with the clothes?"

"No." I was back to my usual attire, dark jeans and boots with a black long-sleeved tee. There were worse things than being called the Terminator. In fact, it was a pretty apt comparison. If only she knew…

I approached the counter, seeing the way her eyes were now guarded.

"Then how can I help you?" Clipped tone. Cautious expression. I knew an angry woman when I saw one.

"Have a drink with me." It was late morning, way past my bedtime, and the only appropriate drink for this time was coffee, when I preferred something stronger. Something told me the answer would be no, but asking her out was my agenda and I stuck to it.

"No."

I waited for an explanation. None came. Just a very firm no.

Interesting. "May I ask why?"

"Does it matter? No means no. Do you not understand that?"

Damn, this woman could boil. "I do understand. But this no is half-assed."

"No," she said coldly. "It's firm."

"That's interesting. So, do you always kneel at a man's dick when taking his measurements? Because I thought I was special."

The hostility in her gaze flickered. It was subtle and quick, but it was there.

"I know you were hitting on me, sweetheart. Not my first rodeo."

"Don't do the sweetheart thing."

"Then don't make me hard just for fun."

"I didn't do that for fun—"

"You did it for research—and I'm sure you liked what you saw."

She kept up her stare, shoulders back, her gaze fierce.

Jesus Christ, I wanted to fuck this woman. "Let's get that drink."

It took her a moment to word her response. "The answer is still no."

It was all heat and flirtatious fun until she came to my apartment. That was the only thing that had changed. Did my wealth intimidate her? I found it hard to believe anything intimidated this woman. "Why?"

She slowly stiffened, as if straightening her spine in anticipation of an attack. "I know what you are."

I blinked as I processed the statement.

Her hands remained on the counter, close to the pen sitting there in case she needed to grab it and jab me in the eye.

The heat between us suddenly turned into tension.

"And what is that?" I finally asked.

Her eyes flicked back and forth between mine. "A criminal."

The corners of my mouth lifted slightly. "What gave me away?"

"The men. The guns."

They'd been discreet, but she was too observant. "I'm not the kind of criminal that hurts people."

"Only those who cross them, right?" she asked coldly. "Like how I'm crossing you right now."

My eyes narrowed. "And I definitely don't hurt women."

For someone who was afraid, she sure didn't look it. "You aren't my type, so just go."

"Then you must be into women because I'm every woman's type."

"Wow." She released a forced laugh. "I don't date criminals."

"Then don't date me."

She held my stare, that undeniable attraction sizzling between us.

"You know what you want from me. The same thing I want from you."

"Which is?"

I said it bluntly, didn't smooth out the edges. "To fuck you."

Now, she broke eye contact altogether, like my intensity became too much for her.

"In the mouth. In the ass. Between your tits. Anywhere I'll fit."

She kept her gaze averted, but the deep breath she took showed her hand. "I don't want to get involved with someone like you." She had to force herself to say it, to override the natural urges screaming inside her body.

"Then don't get involved. One night. That's it."

Her eyes moved to me.

"You can go back to fucking your boring nine-to-five assholes tomorrow."

She remained quiet, her fingers close to the pen sitting on the counter. Throughout the conversation, she'd discreetly moved her hand, getting closer and closer, as if she thought I wouldn't notice. Now, she was close enough to reach it and stab it into my neck, but she didn't bother. "One night."

My dick broke a record, it got hard so fast.

"I mean it."

"One night is all I need, sweetheart."

"And don't call me that. Otherwise, I'll slap you."

"Is that supposed to deter me?" I asked, giving her a partial smile. "I'll see you at eight."

"Where?"

"Your place."

"You know where I live?"

I flashed her a grin before I turned away to walk out. "I'm a criminal, aren't I?"

She lived in a modest apartment. It was in a decent part of Paris, but the building was old and run-down, and I imagined it was a one-bedroom space that was less than four hundred square feet. For a daughter of a billionaire, she was certainly living in squalor. That told me she was on her own entirely, not running up daddy's credit cards to keep herself afloat.

I respected an independent woman.

Was a bit turned on by it, honestly.

I knocked on her door, in my military boots she didn't like, sporting the leather jacket that made me look like a ruthless killer. She mocked my fashion choices, but she still wanted to fuck me, so I guessed I wasn't that bad.

"It's open."

I stepped inside, seeing a small apartment where everything was close together. There was a small kitchen with an island, and the living room contained a single couch that faced a TV on an entertainment center. A deep red rug sat on the hardwood floor, and in the rear, I saw the door that led to the bathroom. Her bedroom must be the other door.

It was small, but her taste in décor at least made it cozy. It matched her outfits, bold but elegant.

She stood in the kitchen and uncorked a bottle of wine.

All she wore was a shiny black robe cinched at her waist. She brought the glass to her lips and took a drink, her eyes on me from across the room. They were smoky with dark eye shadow and thick lashes. Her dark hair was straight this time, reaching past her shoulders to her breasts. When she finished her drink, her red lipstick left a stain.

I loved lipstick stains—just not on glasses.

She carried the glasses to the couch and sat down, her legs crossed, the robe rising a little farther up her sexy legs. She somehow made that robe sexier than lingerie.

I took the seat beside her and reached for the glass she offered me. "You have a nice place."

"Do I?" she asked, seeing straight through my small talk.

"I'm serious."

"My apartment is probably the size of your closet."

"And it'd be a shithole without your taste."

She stilled at my candor then took a drink.

"Something you should know about me…I'll always give it to you straight."

"I don't care about your honesty. I just hope you give other things to me straight…"

I took another drink as I looked at her, a woman all the more stunning because she was ruthless. Her eyes were fierce. Her mouth was brutal. I'd never met another woman like her. Camille was different from other women, but she didn't have this fire. Inferno…that was a better description. "I will."

My arm moved over the back of the couch, and I got comfortable, my knees wide apart, looking at her beside me.

Her eyes held mine, keeping up her look of confidence to mask her unease. She was nervous, her heart pounding under that thin robe. I could see it in the breaths she took. Her chest gave her away.

My hand reached for her knee, soft against my callused fingers. My fingers dipped to the inside of her knee, feeling the softest flesh I'd ever known. My eyes dropped to my movements because the single touch was utterly intoxicating. I trailed up slowly, my fingers opening the robe the farther I moved up her thigh. Olive skin that was as delicate as rose petals. I moved higher up, reaching the apex of her thighs.

My fingers met the satin of black panties.

I loved black.

My thumb found her nub, and I pushed it like a button.

Her response was immediate, sucking in a much-needed breath. Her head tilted back slightly too, and one knee dropped farther away, giving me more room to keep touching her.

I accepted the invitation and touched her harder.

Her breaths slowly built up, becoming deeper, her skin blushing a beautiful pink.

My hand slid to the back of her neck before my fingers fisted that lustrous hair. I slowly moved in, my lips landing on those pink clouds. As my fingers dipped inside her panties, I kissed her, imagining that red lipstick all over my mouth.

Her palm met my cheek, and she deepened the kiss with a swirl of her perfect tongue. It was just the right amount of breath, just the right amount of desperate pant. Her fingers dug into my short hair as she started to grind against my fingers.

She wasn't afraid to show a man what she wanted—and I loved that.

My fingers left her aching sex, and I moved up higher, finding the bow she'd tied at the front of her robe. My fingers gripped the satin ends and slowly pulled it free. Her kiss was exquisite, but I wanted to see the goodies under the robe.

My eyes dropped to a flat tummy with a cute navel piercing. I looked up, seeing the perkiest, sexiest tits I'd ever laid eyes on. "Damn, you're perfect." My hand flattened over her stomach and slowly migrated up, pushing between her plump tits until I gripped one in my bare hand.

My lips landed on her neck, and I kissed her as I squeezed her tit with my hand, feeling the supple softness, flicking the hard nipple with my thumb. My lips trailed down, tasting that delicious skin everywhere, getting that tit in my mouth as fast as I could.

Fuck, this woman was fire.

She was mine now. My body was on top of hers, and I kissed her everywhere. Her neck, her jawline, her collarbone. Both nipples visited my mouth and were moistened by my tongue. My kisses moved in the valley between her tits. I kissed that tight stomach then swirled my tongue around that glittering piercing at her belly button. My thumb hooked into her panties, and she lifted her hips so I could slide them down her long legs.

I didn't eat pussy a lot, but damn, I wasn't leaving until I had a taste.

Mother of God.

My mouth sealed over her heat, and I feasted, tasting pussy that was bold like wine but sweet like strawberries. The combination made a nice flavor on my tongue. My arms were hooked underneath her thighs as I pinned her back, on my knees on the rug, listening to this woman moan and dig her nails into my forearms.

Her ankles locked behind my head, and she ground her body into me, wanting me to eat her alive.

With pleasure, sweetheart.

I focused on her clit and kept swirling, kept pressing, kept digging in my tongue until she started to quiver.

Was she a screamer or a crier? I was about to find out.

Her hips bucked into my face as she writhed on the couch, her moans passing through the thin walls and invading her neighbors' dinner. Her deep voice became high-pitched, hitting a crescendo, and then they came.

The tears.

I got to my feet and lifted her with me, ready for my turn. I moved into her bedroom and found the queen-sized bed against the wall. I dropped her on the bed then stepped back, yanking off my jacket because it felt like a poncho at the moment.

She moved to the edge of the bed and worked my jeans with anxious hands.

I pulled my shirt over my head as she tugged down my jeans and boxers. The shoes came last, because the strings had to be loosened before they came free. I kicked them aside and watched her stare at me, look right at the cock she teased.

I snapped my fingers as I threw my hand down, commanding her to her knees.

In a different context, I'd probably be slapped, but she seemed eager to please me after I'd pleased her so damn good.

She dropped to her knees, her sexy ass supported on the backs of her ankles, and she gripped my thighs as she brought her lips in to kiss me right on the head. Then there was a swirl of her tongue. A breath. Her tongue flattened and she descended, pushing my big dick to the back of her throat.

My hand burrowed in that thick hair, and I pushed until there was nowhere else to go.

I could feel her twitch, like she wanted to gag, but she was clearly a professional because she kept it together.

This exact image had flashed across my mind when she'd measured me in her office, but reality was better than any fantasy. Her eyes were on me as she pulled her mouth to the tip of my dick and pushed in again, stuffing her throat full of big cock. She kept going over and over, slow and steady, taking her time to enjoy it rather than sprinting to get me off.

My hand slid to her cheek and cupped her face, the tips of my fingers digging into her beautiful hair. Her skin was so soft, and I felt myself squeezing her neck harder than I should. Naked in all my glory, like a god above a temple priestess, I fucked her mouth until the saliva pooled in the corners then dripped down her chin.

She'd clearly bitten off more than she could chew, but she still liked it.

Her mouth was great, but her pussy was better.

I pulled my dick out of her mouth, a line of spit stretching between her mouth and my cock.

She was on her feet then on the bed, scooting back toward the headboard.

My knees hit the mattress, and I climbed up, covering that sexy body with my own. My thighs parted her knees, and we came together, her tits against my chest, her hands across my back.

My dick scooped into her entrance.

"You really think I'm going to let you fuck me without protection?" she asked, still a spitfire even when her head was in the clouds. "I know where men like you have been."

Balls deep in whores.

My girls were checked and I was checked, but I wouldn't kill the mood with an argument. I grabbed the rubber from her nightstand, rolled it on as far as it would reach, and then sank in.

Sensations were numbed by the latex between us, but the deeper I went, the better it felt. She was so fucking tight that it made up for the reduced feeling. And nothing could stop me from feeling just how wet she was. One climax wasn't enough. This woman was greedy for more.

I thrust deep and hard, making her gasp right away. The headboard rocked against the wall, the shitty springs in the mattress squeaked, and she moaned against my ear as her ankles hooked around my waist. Her nails clamped down on my back, and she moaned with pleasure, rocking her hips back into me, enjoying the way I nailed her like a whore.

Then she said something that threw me off my game.

"Harder."

Like this wasn't hard enough?

I was a killer on the streets but a gentleman in the bedroom, so I obliged. Every time I thrust inside her, I landed against her clit, hitting that button like it operated a nuclear bomb. Her breaths deepened and her nails sharpened. Once her thighs started to squeeze me and her breathing hitched, I knew I was giving it to her exactly as she wanted.

My lips moved to her ear. "Hard enough for you?"

Her body convulsed, her nails dragging down my back, her moans now cries. She came apart underneath me, the longest climax ever clocked.

Her head hit the pillow, and she tilted it back toward the headboard, new tears streaking to her ears.

The ache for release took over, so I plowed into her hard, achieving a climax that was so good it made my skin catch on fire. I filled the latex but pretended I was pumping into her, giving this beautiful woman a load that would drip down her legs the second she stood on her feet. Our orgasms synced up for a brief time, our moans and cries mixing together in an erotic soundtrack. Then I finished alone, buried deep inside exquisite pussy.

Fuck, that was good.

I rolled off and discarded the rubber before I rolled on another.

Laura's tired eyes suddenly hardened when she saw I was ready to go again—already.

"It's your turn, sweetheart." I patted my thigh. "Show me what you can do."

We lay there in silence for a long time.

Both of us needed a break.

I was a super soldier, but I was still human.

She lay beside me with the sheets kicked to the edge of the bed. Her beautiful body was on display, with a tiny little stomach and big tits. Her long legs were toned, like all that time spent walking in pumps had chiseled her already sexy body.

She must have noticed details of my body too, because she stared at me the entire time.

Now was my chance for pillow talk. "Going in tomorrow?"

"No way. One of the nice things about being your own boss."

It was even nicer to be the boss of an empire. My phone was on silent, because I could do whatever the fuck I wanted.

"You don't seem tired."

"I work nights."

Her hand slid across the sheets toward me until her fingertips rested against the scar on my stomach. "Were you shot?"

She knew her scars. "Yes."

"Did you deserve it?"

The corner of my mouth rose in a smile. "Hundred percent."

"Did you kill the man who did this to you?"

"No." I wished I had a cigar right now. A drink on the nightstand too.

"Then he must be your friend."

"I don't have friends. But if I did…he would be one of them."

Her fingers continued to caress my scar. "Are you ever going to wear the clothes I picked out for you?"

I gave a slight shrug.

"So the only reason you walked into my store was to fuck me?"

Not the only reason. "Why else would I let you insult me?"

"I didn't insult you," she said with a smile. "Just trying to give you some pointers."

"You liked the way I looked, so maybe I don't need any pointers."

"Touché." Her hand moved up to my hard chest, mapping out the details of my body.

"Have you lived in Paris all your life?"

"No."

"I can tell by your accent."

"Then why did you ask?"

The corner of my mouth rose in a smile again. "Where are you from?"

"Florence."

"The birthplace of the Renaissance. You remind me of those paintings."

"The ones where women are draped over couches with their tits hanging out?"

"Exactly."

She released a little laugh, and the sound was nice. "I'll take that as a compliment."

"You should." I stared at her beside me, loving those sexy hips. She had an hourglass figure. Unbelievable. I felt my dick start to harden after its reprieve. "Did your family move here with you?"

Without flinching whatsoever, she answered the question. "No."

"So, your parents are still in Italy?"

"Not my mother."

"Where is she?"

"Dead." She said it without emotion, like she couldn't care less. Or it was just a front to mask her unbearable pain.

"I'm sorry." I'd never had parents, so I could never really understand the loss. "At least you have your father."

"Ha." She released a sarcastic laugh. "Not really."

Now I was right where I wanted. "You don't get along?"

"We don't speak."

"How long has that been going on?"

"Seven years."

"I'm sorry."

Her eyes were still hard, completely callous.

"May I ask why?"

Her eyes remained steady, like she'd zoned out during our conversation. "He's an asshole. That's why."

I knew that was the end of the conversation, so I didn't press it.

"What about you?"

After my interrogation, I was obligated to answer. "I was a surprise to my parents. I was more than they could handle, so they dropped me off in an orphanage. I was two years old, so I don't remember them."

She turned to look at me, her eyes sympathetic.

"I left the orphanage when I was sixteen. Got involved with the wrong crowd but made the right connections. Rose through the ranks, killed anyone who got in my way, and now I run the biggest drug empire in France."

Her eyes remained steady.

"Guess we have something in common... My dad's an asshole too."

"Have you ever reconnected with them?"

"No," I said with a slight laugh. "I tracked them down to kill them in their sleep. But then shit got in the way."

"What kind of shit?"

"Kids."

Her eyebrows furrowed.

"You heard me right, sweetheart. They had two kids after they left me in the orphanage. Never came back for me. Never had a second thought." I said it all with a slight smile on my lips, finding the sad story a bit funny. "I didn't want those kids to end up like me, so I left them in peace."

She seemed stunned by that information because she just stared for a long time. "How old were they?"

"Early teens. This was almost ten years ago."

She fell silent, like she didn't know what to say.

"Does your dad seem like less of an asshole now?"

Her eyes found mine again, hardened by an impenetrable mask. "It's not a competition."

Her gaze exuded power. It was the brightness, but it was also the confidence. She could command attention with just a look, make someone feel small with only that potent stare. It was addictive—being the recipient of that gaze. I'd never seen a woman wear confidence like she owned it.

Most of the company I kept were whores. Women paid to do what they were told. There was limited pillow talk. I didn't pick up women in bars because civilians were boring. It was just easier to throw down a wad of cash and bark out orders. When I met Camille, I found her interesting, but she was nothing compared to this lion.

I felt my hardness creep in the longer I stared at her. I had yet to take her from behind, that ass in my face, but I was so enraptured by those eyes that I didn't want to look away. I wanted to watch her reaction to every touch.

When I moved on top of her, she moved with me, like she'd been waiting for me to make the move ever since she noticed my hardness return. Her fingers fisted my hair instantly, and her lips found mine with an unspent hunger.

I ground my dick against her clit, getting her sex ready for another pounding. She had to be sore by now, but her desire for another climax outweighed the rawness between her legs.

I rolled on another condom and entered her in a single thrust.

She gasped against my lips, her legs straight against my chest with her ankles on my shoulders. Her hands gripped my ass, nails sharp.

This time, she didn't need to tell me how she wanted it.

I fucked her as hard as I could—and listened to how loud I made her come.

It was four in the morning when she walked me to the door.

That black robe was cinched around her waist, her naked body hidden from view under the thin material. Her hair and makeup were a mess, which told me I had carried out a job well done. She opened the door then waited for me to walk out. "Goodbye, Bartholomew."

The transaction was completed. The one-night stand had concluded.

But I'd never wanted one to end less. "Good night, sweetheart." I walked up to her and watched her eyes immediately dip to my lips. My nose rubbed up against hers, bringing her eyes back to mine. We stared, the heat still between us like the night of fucking didn't extinguish it. I gave her a kiss, my eyes open, watching the way she enjoyed it after I'd already kissed her everywhere.

I pulled away and walked out the door. "Maybe I'll see you around."

"Maybe." She started to shut the door. "But I hope not."

4

BARTHOLOMEW

I sat on my throne in the Catacombs, a drink in my hand.

A week had passed since my midnight rendezvous. The ache for more had been hot in my veins ever since, but I told myself that within a week, I'd forget all about her like I did everyone else.

I was wrong about that.

It was like a fire that couldn't be controlled. It burned everything inside me. My skin still felt as if it was ablaze like it did in her bed. My life was about work. Had been that way since I could remember. So I never had one of those booty-call types of relationships. Never had a fling with a woman I met at a bar. My body was satisfied by the dirty shit I did with whores, and it'd always been enough.

But not anymore.

"Bartholomew?"

My eyes refocused on Bleu in front of me. "Yes?"

He faltered, his eyes switching back and forth between mine, like he'd already said a great deal and I'd missed all of it. "You seem distracted."

"Because I am."

Bleu faltered again, like he didn't expect me to admit it. "Want me to do something about it?"

"No." For once in my life, it was a good distraction.

"Are you done having fun with the Skull King's daughter? Because I think she could be of use to us."

The fun was over. I didn't owe her anything at this point. When I captured her, she would be livid, but she'd also understand it wasn't personal. But I still didn't want to do that, because once I did…there was no going back. "No."

Bleu did his best to mask his annoyance. "We've discovered the bulk of the product is shipped from Morocco on

Freightliner trucks on cargo ships. Once it stops at the port in the south of Italy, it drives to Florence. They move a million pounds every two weeks. The Skull King disperses it across his distribution channels, and it reaches the hands of his customers in every corner of the country."

"So if we intercept that ship, we cut off his supply."

"Yes."

"Or better yet, we hit the source directly. Pay them to sell to us exclusively."

"That'll just piss off the Skull King."

"Sure. But without business, he'll start to hurt. His men will start to turn on him."

"I find that unlikely, because we wouldn't turn on you."

The corner of my mouth rose in a smile. "Don't be naïve. We're all wolves here."

Bleu stared.

"I'll make a deal with him. I'll sell him the product he needs, and in return, I get a cut of his business."

Bleu worked it all out in his head. "Not only will you take the territory, but you'll take his distribution network."

"Exactly."

"What if he doesn't cooperate?"

"Then I'll kill his daughter. He'll have no other choice."

Bleu turned quiet for a while. "What if she's not worth it to him? Have you discovered the strain in their relationship?"

I'd gleaned nothing from that woman. Not even a hunch. "No." But she had a backbone of steel and a smile of sunshine. No way any man wouldn't do anything for her—especially her father. "Let's figure out who's in charge of manufacturing. Then we'll make our move."

He nodded before he turned away. "Got it."

5

LAURA

I had just finished making dinner and carried it to the small circular dining table near the window. I poured myself a glass of wine and set up my laptop in front of me. Just because I wasn't at the office didn't mean I didn't have paperwork that required my attention. The business didn't do well enough for me to hire employees, so I worked all the time, like an American.

Just when I got comfortable, someone knocked on the door.

I didn't expect any visitors or packages, so I stayed quiet and waited for them to leave.

Knock. Knock. Knock.

I sighed before I crossed the room, wearing leggings and a sweater that exposed one shoulder. Since I was home without company, I ditched the bra. Because what kind of woman wore a bra when she was home?

I glanced through the peephole.

"What the...?" It was Bartholomew. At my apartment. Without an invitation. In his signature black look, he looked like a shadow that had crawled straight out of the darkness. The sun was just about to set, so it must have been the start of his day. "Why are you here?"

"I'd rather talk to you instead of the door."

"Well, the door's gonna have to do because you have no business being here." He hadn't left anything behind, so he hadn't returned to claim forgotten items. He was there for another purpose—a purpose I wouldn't entertain.

"You think I can't get past this flimsy piece of wood?"

"I'm sure you can. But you can't get past me."

A full grin moved on to his handsome face, unable to contain his amusement. "You have a way with words that really gets to me." The peephole limited my vision, but he seemed to slide his hands into the pockets of his jacket, getting comfortable outside my door.

He wasn't going anywhere.

I took a deep breath and sighed before I let him in.

His eyes locked on mine the second he could see me. The smile had already disappeared, and now I met the intense stare that had caught my attention when he'd stepped into my shop. I should have known what he was then, because a man didn't command the room like that unless he was *somebody*. Somebody who wasn't afraid to ruffle feathers, to tell people what to do, to say what others didn't want to hear. He entered my apartment and shut the door behind him, his boots distinct on my hardwood.

I already felt like I was out of my element the second we breathed the same air—and he was in *my* apartment. It'd been over a week since we'd said goodbye. A long night of good sex that filled my tank all the way. I knew I shouldn't have gotten involved with him, even just for the night, but it'd certainly been worth it.

But now, I wasn't so sure.

He glanced at the table. "Am I interrupting?"

"Are you looking for an invitation?"

He stepped closer to me, tall and slender, smelling like pine and soap...and gunpowder. It was a very specific smell you wouldn't recognize unless you'd been around it your entire life...like I had. "If your cooking tastes anything like your pussy, then yes."

I hid my reaction as best as I could, but I struggled. Only a man like him could pull off a line like that. Why did all the good fucks come from bad guys? I went for the same type of guy over and over. I'd done it again when I'd kneeled right at his cock to get those measurements I didn't even need in the first place. I could figure it out just by looking at him. He had the measurements of a model. The height at over six feet. The broad, masculine shoulders. The body fat percentage that was less than six percent.

I walked away to the stove and made him a plate. Then I placed it across from me at the table.

He approached the chair and stared at the plate. A piece of chicken breast sauteed in a white wine sauce with a side of mashed potatoes and broccolini. "A woman who knows how to fuck and cook... I'm a lucky man." His eyes lifted to me as he dropped his coat off his shoulders and arms. He set it on the back of the chair and took a seat, his strong arms on display in the black t-shirt he wore. Cords ran up his ripped arms and the sides of his neck. The guy must live on a strict diet of only meat and booze to look like that.

I took a seat too, our eyes now level. I closed the laptop between us then cut into my chicken.

He helped himself to my glass of wine.

We ate in silence, like we were on a very tense first date.

He stared at me the entire time, especially when he chewed his food. "Where'd you learn?"

"To cook?" I asked. "Or to fuck?"

That half grin spread across his cheeks, softening the hardness of his face. "Both."

"The internet for cooking. And experience for fucking."

We ate for another stretch of silence, exchanging looks across the table.

"How's work?" he asked.

"Busy. As the sole employee, it never ends. How's the drug empire?"

"Good," he said. "But it's always good."

"You know drugs ruin people's lives, right?"

"Really?" He gave a slight shrug. "It's only made mine better."

"Then you aren't a user."

"Anymore."

My eyes took in his face with deeper clarity.

"I grew up in an orphanage. What did you expect?"

"When did you get clean?"

He looked away, like he was trying to do the math in his head. "Probably ten years. You can't run the show if you're high all the time."

"Well, whatever your reason…good for you."

"What about you?" he asked. "You seem to have a wild side."

"No drugs for me. I don't need that shit to have a good time."

"I like that answer." He refilled the communal wineglass and took a drink. He finished his plate, leaving a single streak of sauce. "Thank you for dinner."

"You mean breakfast?"

His eyes softened slightly in that hard face. High cheekbones. Sharp jawline. Dark hair and dark eyes. He was the definition of tall, dark, and handsome. And he was a little scary too...the way his eyes burned me sometimes.

"Now that we got the small talk out of the way...why are you here?"

"Small talk?" His voice was so deep, deeper than the darkness of his clothing. "If that's what it was, it's the first time I've ever enjoyed it."

I grabbed the glass between us and took a drink. "We agreed it was a one-time thing."

"No deal is ironclad. There's always room to negotiate."

"Not with me." If the circumstances were different, I would have caved the second I opened the door. There was no mistaking the fact that he was one in a million. He was the supreme lord of fucking. I'd be his fuck buddy anytime. Put him at number one on my speed dial for booty calls. God, he was so good-looking it hurt to stare directly at him. But I stayed strong because...I'd been down this road before.

The silence stretched on infinitely. That intense stare pierced me across the table, hard as marble, impenetrable as concrete. He had the best poker face in the world, because it was literally impossible to guess what he was thinking. He didn't even let his emotions fill the room like smoke you could breathe. This man had the discipline of a monk. That was probably why he was so successful in his line of business. "Why?"

"I don't owe you an explanation."

"Yes, you do."

Both eyebrows rose to the top of my head. "Excuse me?"

"When we fuck the way we do, damn right, you owe me an explanation." He straightened and placed his arms on the table, getting closer to me, almost like he was threatening me. "Don't act like your fingers haven't slipped into your panties night after night pretending to be me."

I kept my own poker face, but I felt a jolt of fear at the accusation.

"I'm not watching you." He answered the question I was too proud to ask. "But I know because I've done the same thing. So, explain it to me—or fuck me."

Thankfully, my heart was impossible to see under skin and bone, because he would see how it panicked. My lungs strained for more air, but I did my best to keep it controlled, to beat this sex god at our invisible game of cards. "You're a criminal. You kill people—"

"Only when they deserve it."

"Don't you think that's a bit subjective?"

"And the law isn't?" he asked. "You know, in America, they let guilty people go and put innocent people to death all the time. They have the highest rate of incarceration in the world. But I'm the bad guy?"

"Your world knowledge doesn't impress me."

"How I earn my money and who I put to death have nothing to do with you."

"I'm guessing you've never done this before." I grabbed the glass and took a drink just to cool my nerves.

Bartholomew stared, like he wasn't sure how to respond. "What, exactly?"

"Monogamy."

A slow smile crept on to his lips. "Sweetheart, let's not get ahead of ourselves here—"

"You're working this hard to fuck me with a condom? Let's be real here. Monogamy and commitment are two different things. But what happens when someone notices you spend your nights with a single person rather than a cycle of whores? They come for me because they think I'm important to you. I'm hung in the middle of my living room with slit wrists until you walk in the door and discover me."

Bartholomew was silent, as if he could see the imagery in his head.

"I enjoyed that night together. Do I wish it could happen again? Absolutely. But it's not worth the risk—not when you are what you are."

He seemed to have nothing to say because his eyes shifted to the window, looking at the city lights as they contrasted against the darkness.

I waited for him to leave.

"I'm sorry."

A warmth moved through my stomach like I'd drunk too much wine.

His eyes shifted back to me. "For what happened to you."

My eyes were locked on his, doing my best to remain stoic.

"But that wouldn't happen with me. I'm at the top of the food chain, and I don't have any enemies."

"You do realize those two statements are contradictory, right? You can't be at the top without everyone watching."

"They can watch all they want. Doesn't mean they can touch me."

I released a quiet sigh. "We can talk about this all night, but my answer won't change."

He sank back into the chair, his eyes slowly darkening into disappointment. "You're a stubborn woman."

"I'm an *Italian* woman. It's in my nature."

He gave a slight smile. "You're bold like your wine... I like it."

The conversation seemed to have come to an end, and now all he needed to do was walk out the door.

But he stayed. "We could meet in secret. Under aliases at hotels. I could keep up pretenses with my whores. Whoever you think is watching wouldn't suspect a thing. This relationship would be a bonfire. It would burn white-hot instantly, but slowly, it would die out to embers. In other words, it wouldn't last long." His eyes gripped me from across the table, like his hands gripped my arms and kept me close to him. "Burn with me, sweetheart."

He grabbed the back of his shirt and pulled it over his head. His skin was fair like he hadn't seen daylight in years, but it was still beautiful, the way it was firm over all the individual muscles. The man was ripped, his skin so tight that his veins were visible from his wrists to his shoulders. His defined abs dropped down to a V that led to the top of his jeans. Those dark eyes locked on mine, like he was the predator and I was the prey.

It was uncommon for me to freeze, but I froze when he looked at me like that, like he was cruel—just not to me. His arm circled my waist, and he tugged me into him, his lips landing on my neck like he had the teeth of a vampire. His kiss was hard and hot, tasting my flesh with his tongue.

I melted instantly, enveloped in this man's power. My arms linked around his neck as I let him devour me, take away whatever drop of common sense I had left.

He abruptly turned me around and slammed my back into his chest. The kisses continued as his arm hooked over my stomach. His other hand slid down the front of my leggings, underneath my panties, and then reached my clit. The initial touch was delicate, his fingers gently playing with my nub as he kissed my neck. Then he rubbed me harder, getting my back to arch against him, my hand to grip his forearm because it felt so good. His lips came to my ear. "Is this how you touch yourself?" He rubbed me harder and listened to my pants grow louder. "When you think of me?"

I felt his hand slide up my shirt and grip my tits. He squeezed one before he grazed my nipple with his thumb. The feel of his bare chest to my back, the depth of his voice in my ear, his strong fingers in my panties…it all made me feel like a lit stick of dynamite. "Yes…"

I could feel him smile against my ear.

He yanked my shirt over my head then grabbed both of my tits with his hands. He gave them each a firm squeeze before he pulled my leggings down. He kneeled with the fabric then forced me to bend over so he could kiss me there.

I held on to the end of the bed as I felt his tongue swirl around me. Over and over. Bringing me to the edge. The spark came closer, almost hitting the dynamite to make me explode into pieces.

But then it stopped. "Bartholomew…"

He dropped his jeans to his thighs. "I'm coming, sweetheart." He ripped the packet, rolled it on, and then grabbed both of my hips before he shoved himself inside.

My moan was practically a scream. God, I loved that dick. It hurt—but it felt so good.

His hand flattened against my stomach, and he brought me into him, having me sit on top of him slightly as we both kneeled on the rug around my bed. He ground into me, feeling our bodies move together, all the while feeling me up and rubbing my clit at the same time. "Nothing can stop this." His lips were at my ear, his voice so deep that it turned me on even more. "Not even you."

6

BARTHOLOMEW

We took a seat at the circular table. Except for the two of us, every seat was empty.

Camille sat beside me, dressed in a beautiful black dress, her hair styled nicely. On her left hand, a diamond ring sparkled. It blew our story, but I didn't ask her not to wear it. If people thought I was fucking a married woman, that was right in line with my image.

"You seem distracted."

I'd been staring into the crowd, at nothing in particular. "I'm thinking."

"About?"

Pussy. One, in particular. "My drugs are crossing into Croatia, but now I have my eyes set on another territory."

"Italy," she said. "I remember."

"I'm trying to make that happen, but it's complicated."

"You could not make it happen," she said. "You've got all of France and now Croatia."

I issued a quiet laugh.

"What?"

"Just because your husband copped out easily doesn't mean I will." I continued to stare at the mingling guests at the dinner, waiting for my opportunity to speak with the French diplomat. I successfully imported the drugs across the border, but it was a costly endeavor. If I could get shipping regulations changed, it would make my life easier.

Camille stared hard at the side of my face. I could feel her attitude like a wildfire. "Let me ask you something."

"This should be good…"

"How much money do you have?"

I released a quiet chuckle. "Wouldn't you like to know…"

"I'm guessing it's billions?"

I didn't answer.

"You have all this money, and you can't even spend it. What's the point? To pay in cash when you're at the gas pump? To have free groceries for the rest of your life?"

I tore my gaze away from the crowd and looked directly at her. "Because we have these little rendezvous, you think you know everything about me. But in fact, you don't know me at all. And you definitely don't know a damn thing about my money."

That shut her up.

"I own a hundred different businesses across Paris. Restaurants, storage facilities, gyms, bars, everything you can think of. That's how I wash my money. And that's how my guys are paid on the books so they can put their kids in private school and whatever bullshit they want."

"How do you manage all that?"

"I've got people."

She seemed slightly overwhelmed by that information. "Then let me rephrase my question. What's the point in doing more when you're already a billionaire? At what point will it be enough?"

I looked away again. "It's not about the money, Camille."

"Then what is it about?"

I let the silence linger even though my answer was on the tip of my tongue. "Power."

"Doesn't that get old?"

"Does sex get old?" I looked at her again. "Does looking out at the ocean from your terrace get old? Does flying in your private plane get old?"

She was quiet.

"No." I answered for her.

"Regimes rise and fall every day. The Roman Empire was untouchable…and look where they are now."

"But they're remembered. They're revered."

She released a quiet sigh. "I'm sorry, Bartholomew. You won't be mentioned in history books."

"Maybe. Maybe not."

"I just don't see the point in all this, especially when you have a target on your back."

"Anyone would be stupid to fuck with me."

"Cauldron and Grave are powerful men, but someone crossed them."

"We aren't the same, sweetheart." The comparison was borderline offensive.

"What happens when you get older? What will you have then?"

I looked at her, locking my gaze on to hers. "I didn't invite you here to interrogate me. And I certainly didn't invite you here to judge me."

"I'm doing neither of those things. I just care about you."

"Care about me?" I almost laughed because it was such a strange sentence.

"Yes."

"I told you I don't have friends."

"Then what are we?"

"Business acquaintances."

"I think we're more than that if we're having this conversation."

"We aren't having it," I said. "You're forcing it."

"You never answered my question," she said. "What will happen when you get older?"

"Get older?" I asked. "There's no such thing in this line of work. There's no retirement. You die young—as you should."

"Dying young...that doesn't scare you?"

"Not one bit."

"So, a wife and a family... Not your thing?"

"Having me as a husband would be torture. And my kids would hate me."

She watched me, her eyes dissecting me.

"Are we done with this conversation now?" I asked. "Because we have shit to do."

"Yeah...I guess."

7

LAURA

I was on the phone when a guy walked into the office.

I say *guy* because he definitely wasn't a client. Just like Bartholomew, he was dressed all in black, like he worked the streets all night and was about to finish his shift at ten in the morning.

"Anne, let me call you back."

Without saying a word, he placed a sealed package on the counter. There was no writing on the outside. Then he walked out and disappeared as quickly as he'd arrived.

I pulled out the papers Bartholomew had sent me.

The first was his medical clearance, results from his STI panel, proving that he kept his dick clean. The test had been performed at some lab facility, and I found it funny to imagine Bartholomew walking in there…looking like Bartholomew. He probably had his own doctor on staff, but to assure me he didn't alter the results, he'd gone somewhere neutral.

There was also a note along with a hotel key.

Four Seasons

Room 822

8 p.m.

That was all it said.

This was such a bad idea. No matter how good the sex was, it wasn't worth getting pulled into his darkness. It wasn't worth having his cronies swing by my office. It wasn't worth all the risk.

But I'd dated on and off for years, and only the bad ones knew how to do it good.

The hotel was the epitome of luxury. Flowers on every table. Gold elevators. Glass staircases. I stepped into the elevator and hit the button to reach the eighth floor, looking at my image in the sea of gold.

My heart was like a fucking race car.

I'd fucked this man twice, and yet, it felt like the first time.

No man had ever made me so nervous. Made my heart pump with adrenaline. Made me a little afraid to be in his presence.

The doors opened, and I stepped into the carpeted hallway. At the end of the hall was the room I was looking for, crystal chandelier on the way, low-lit scones along the walls that looked like singing angels.

I swiped the card over the door and stepped inside.

It was a master suite, with an entryway, a grand living room, and a private bedroom at the other side. My heels tapped against the hardwood as I made my entrance. I headed to the floor-to-ceiling windows at the back, the Eiffel Tower on full display.

I took in the view as I waited for him to arrive. I expected someone like him to be punctual, so I pulled out my phone to check the time. He was ten minutes late. I turned to set my purse on the counter but stilled when I spotted him in the armchair.

Knees wide apart. Elbows on the armrests. His big hands together. He'd been sitting there watching me the entire time, and judging by the intensity in his eyes, he'd enjoyed the view.

Something about this man made me go absolutely still. I had no voice. No control over my body. I never let a man take my power, but Bartholomew stole it straight from my hands. I did my best to keep my breathing even, to keep my stare hard, to pretend he didn't affect me the way he did.

I hoped he bought it.

After a long stare, he rose to his feet. His jacket was already on the back of the chair, and he wore a short-sleeved shirt that showed all that arm porn. With the confidence of a Roman emperor, he walked right up to me, lowered his face to mine, his lips hovering just inches away, and then he stared.

I could barely breathe.

His hand cupped my cheek then slid into my hair, and as he spoke, his eyes dropped to my lips. "I've thought about you all day, sweetheart." He cradled the back of my head as he kissed me, a gentle kiss that sent shivers everywhere. Each was soft and delicate, a quiet simmer on the stove, the heat slowly rising and bringing us to a boil. His mouth opened fully and took mine, his tongue entering my mouth to claim its victory.

At some point, my fingers had dug into his hair, and my hand clutched his strong shoulder. My heart raced in excitement rather than fear, and I fell into this sweet oblivion without reserve.

My hands gripped the bottom of his shirt and tugged it over his head. Once my palms felt his bare skin, it was like touching the sun. Searing heat moved through my extremities to my center, the transfer of heat happening at the speed of electricity.

He pulled my shirt off next and unclasped my bra with a single hand. Once the material fell, he squeezed both of my tits with his hands and moaned into my mouth. He must be a tit man, because he grabbed on to them every chance he could.

He guided me backward to the bed, popping my jeans open and tugging them down over my ass as we moved.

The master bedroom was decorated in a rosy blush and crystal. A large mural was on the wall, depicting ancient times. We both got naked from the waist down and made it onto the bed. When my back hit the soft sheets, I realized he had already stripped back the covers so we could fuck without interruption.

He was clearly in a hurry to fuck me without a condom because he didn't go down on me like he usually did. He went straight for the kill, separating my thighs with his and guiding himself in with a smooth entry.

I didn't need any foreplay anyway. The sight of his naked body was more than enough foreplay for me.

His eyes burned into mine as he sank deep, giving a quiet moan under his breath when he felt skin-on-skin. "Fuck."

Yes, fuck. Perfect word to describe it.

He fucked me like he'd never had the pleasure before. Hard and aggressive, pounding into me as he supported one of my legs with his arm. The hard muscles of his chest and shoulders started to gleam with sweat, but he pressed on like he had the endurance of an ultramarathoner.

My only job was to lie there and let him fuck me.

God, I was a lucky woman.

His arm suddenly scooped under the small of my back, and he brought us together differently, rubbing his pelvis right against my clit over and over, his big dick pulsing inside me.

He seemed to know I was all about the clit, because he ground into me over and over, thrusting inside me with deep and even strokes, making my legs start to tremble because I knew he was purposely trying to make me come.

Most men never even bothered to try.

My nails clawed his back, and I thrust along with him, my head rolling back the moment it started. It was all too much, the feel of his body on top of mine, the shadows in the bedroom, the sounds of our moans and the slickness of our wet bodies, the fact that this was a clandestine meeting in a hotel like star-crossed lovers. I came, and I came hard, probably harder than I ever had.

He wouldn't let me look away as I rode the throes of inexplicable pleasure. His hand fisted my hair and anchored me in position, sitting in the front row of my tearful production. He watched the whole thing, his dick thickening inside me in anticipation of his release.

"Always look at the man who makes you come." His fingers tightened on the back of my neck as he continued to fuck me.

Tears streaked down my cheeks to my ears, and my nails clawed his back the way a cat shredded a throw pillow. My hand gripped his ass, and I tugged him into me. "Come inside me." I tugged on him again and again. The climax was over, but the heat still burned between my legs. "You've earned it."

He reacted quicker than the flip of a light switch, his hips bucking out of rhythm, his moans more like growls from a wolf. The cords in his neck tightened, and his jawline became sharper than cut glass when he clenched his teeth like that. His normally fair skin was tinted red with exertion and desire, and he pumped into me like a man desperate to mark his territory.

I could feel it inside me. Feel the weight. Feel the heat.

He came to a stop, his dick still so hard it was clear that climax didn't make a dent.

Both breathing hard, we looked at each other, our bodies tangled together, the heat between us still burning us alive.

"How would you like me to fuck you next, sweetheart?"

I didn't reject the endearment. He could call me whatever he wanted when he made me come like that. "Like this." I disentangled myself from his body and pressed my cheek into the bed, my ass straight to the ceiling. My head was close to my knees, deepening the angle in my back as far as I could.

His knees dipped the mattress as he scooted closer to me. His hand grabbed both of my wrists and pinned them against the small of my back. Then his big dick entered me like a wrecking ball against a building about to be demolished. "Good choice."

The bed was so comfortable. I hadn't slept on sheets like this for quite a while. Luxury used to be a basic part of my existence, but it'd been so long since I'd had nice things that I'd forgotten how wonderful it was to have them.

He lay beside me, the sheets down at his waist, his arm propped behind his head as he looked out at the view.

There was a foot of space between us, both of us hot and sweaty from the hours he'd spent buried deep inside me.

He reached for the nightstand, took a drink of his scotch, and then grabbed the cigar he'd set there. "You mind?"

"I like the way they smell."

He grabbed the lighter and lit up. "Didn't expect you to say that."

"Well, it looked like you were going to do it anyway, regardless of what I said."

He smiled before he pulled a cloud of smoke into his mouth, letting the taste coat his tongue. After several seconds, he released, the smoke rising in the air and momentarily blocking our view of the lights.

We lay there in comfortable silence. The smell made me think of fonder memories, my dad smoking by the pool while my mother flipped through a magazine. I had a popsicle in my mouth. Lemon was my flavor.

He handed the cigar to me.

"No thanks."

He brought it back to his lips and took another puff.

I pulled the sheets farther up my body and tried not to fall asleep. Wasn't sure how I could be so comfortable with the biggest drug kingpin in France. It was easy to forget what he really was when he was everything else I'd ever wanted.

"Was it your father?"

My head turned to him, seeing him looking sexy as hell in the limited light. If I weren't raw, I'd be on top of him right now. "Was what my father?"

"The one who smoked cigars."

He was right on the money. "Yes."

"So he wasn't always an asshole…"

"Or I was just too young to realize it at the time."

Silence trickled by for a while. "No chance you two will ever make up?"

"No."

"Family is everything to Italians. May I ask what he did?"

I looked at the city lights as I considered my answer. "We don't have to do the pillow talk thing."

"That's too bad because I enjoy your company."

"Really?" I asked, finding that interesting.

He turned to look at me. "Why is that so surprising?"

"You don't seem like a talker."

"Guess you bring out a different side of me." He continued to smoke his cigar and looked out the window. "My men are loyal to me. I'm always surrounded by a sea of people. Women are in my bed constantly. But I can honestly tell you I don't have a single friend. Well… except one. And he'd probably tell you otherwise." He gave a quiet chuckle.

I wasn't the least bit surprised. You couldn't make friends in that line of work. "You'd better not be friend-zoning me right now…"

He broke into a quick laugh, his chest rumbling with the sound. "I could never be friends with a woman with an ass like yours." He took a final puff of his cigar then smashed it in the crystal ashtray on the nightstand. "I should get going. Got a lot on the docket tonight." He rose from the bed, six-foot-something, all man.

Why didn't good men ever look like that? I lay back on the pillow, too comfortable to ever move.

He looked at me when I didn't rise. "You can sleep here if you want."

"I just might."

He cracked a smile. "Have breakfast in the morning."

"Ooh, that means no dishes."

His eyes continued to look amused.

I propped my head on one arm then patted the empty bed beside me.

He stood there, his eyes flicking to the spot where I wanted him.

"One more…before you go."

Instead of giving me that arrogant smile, he consumed me whole with that stare. His knees hit the bed, and then he was on top of me, his lips sealing over mine as his big hand grabbed my ass and gave it a squeeze. "Yes, sweetheart."

8

BARTHOLOMEW

I got busy at work.

There was a little organization on the streets of Paris that was selling my premium shit at an even higher premium. I thought I'd killed the rats, but of course, there was another nest...and then another nest. Most of the big bosses in the business ignored the little guys selling a couple ounces a week.

But not me.

I was the one and only.

I also had a partnership with Hell. I had become the lead distributor of their acid, taking a small fee because I'd done it as a favor—to get Claire back. The relationship was ongoing and took up my time. Sometimes it required my attention outside of Paris, and I would be gone for days at a time.

But I hadn't forgotten Laura.

She was always on my mind, and sometimes I could still feel her warm tits in my hand when I closed my eyes. I was always open for business, but she revved up my engine to critical levels that couldn't be satisfied with a whore. Even if we hadn't been monogamous, any other woman would be a knock-off of the real thing.

The second I returned to Paris, Bleu had news for me.

"We located the manufacturer. In the mountains in the south of Marrakech. They have a full enterprise there, a lab underground so the government can't see it on satellite. I was able to connect with people aware of its existence, but no one who can get me a meeting."

"At least it's progress. Good luck, Bleu." I took a seat on the throne. "How's Benton?"

He gave a shrug. "Haven't talked much."

I saw his brother's eyes whenever I looked at him. Steel blue. "You know how newlyweds can get."

"I don't think that's what it is…"

I knew what it was.

"He wants to protect his family... I get it." After a long stare, he turned away. "I'll let you know when I find out more."

I want to see you, sweetheart.

I hope you want to do a lot more than that.

Every time I read her messages, I heard that beautiful voice in my head, felt her fire through the words. It made the withdrawals all that more intense. *Meet me at our place.* We didn't need to operate in such secrecy, like this was a clandestine affair that could break up two marriages. No one was watching me. No one was watching her. But if that's what she wanted, so be it.

That's our place now?

I thought you'd prefer to be fucked in a palace instead of a dirty motel room.

I don't know...a sketchy room on the wrong side of town could be fun.

I sucked air through my teeth and felt my dick give a twitch in my jeans. *I can't wait to fuck that mouth.*

Don't forget to fuck my other goodies too.

Other goodies? *You're torturing me.*

It's called dirty talk.

Be careful, sweetheart. You don't know who you're dealing with.

Then hurry up and show me.

I clenched my jaw and squeezed the phone in my hand. I was parked outside the apartment, light raindrops hitting the windows, and the hard-on in my jeans was so thick I had to unbutton the top to give it extra room.

Then I had to wait a solid five minutes until I could walk up to the door and knock.

Benton answered the door, his steely eyes regarding me with a hint of coldness.

"You going to invite me in, or…?"

He seemed to debate with himself for a minute before he opened the door. "Just keep it down. Claire is asleep."

Benton and I sat in the living room in front of the fire, the same room where Benton had told me his daughter was not dead, as he'd feared. Now we shared a decanter of scotch in the armchairs, sitting across from each other as the rain continued to come down.

Benton rested his chin on his closed knuckles, his eyes on the glass decanter on the table between us. "Still moving forward with that idiot plan of yours?"

"Which one? You think they're all idiot plans."

His eyes hardened. "The Skull King."

"Yes, plan is still underway."

Benton looked like he had a whole lot to say but chose not to say it.

"We found his manufacturer. We're going to cut him off at the source. Make him work for us."

"And you actually think that will work?"

"Why wouldn't it?"

"Because this is the Skull King. He's your equal. Would you work for someone else?"

I refilled my glass. "Maybe initially."

"It's like you want to get killed."

"Wouldn't be the worst thing in the world," I said before I took another drink. "But that's not the reason for my visit tonight."

"So it gets better…" He rubbed his palms together, his elbows on his knees.

I crossed my legs, letting one ankle rest on the opposite knee. It would be easy to rush this conversation and sprint to the hotel to shove my dick in Laura's mouth, but business came first. "Bleu says you don't talk much anymore."

Benton lifted his head higher and looked at me. "My relationship with my brother is none of your concern."

"Is it because he works for me?"

Benton never answered.

"That's not fair, Benton."

"It's not who he works *for*. It's who he associates with."

"You think you're better than us? Let's not forget the only reason you're sitting there is because a condom ripped."

"You want me to shoot you again?"

The grin that entered my face was unstoppable. "Don't ghost your brother. He's the only family you've got left."

"I have a family—a wife and a daughter."

"You know what I mean. Just because he earns his money in criminal ways doesn't mean he shouldn't be able to come over here and spend time with you and Claire. If someone wants to make something happen, they'll go after me. Bleu is just a foot soldier. I'm the commander. He's not going to lead trouble to your doorstep. He's not going to get Claire taken."

Benton dropped his gaze and looked at the decanter. "I wish he hadn't gotten involved…"

"I don't blame the guy for wanting riches. We all do."

"But it comes at a hefty price."

"What price is that? Because I haven't paid a dime."

He lifted his gaze and looked at me again. "You don't see it."

"See what?"

"What it's done to you."

My eyes locked on his face, not blinking, just staring. "What's it done to me?"

Benton looked at the fire, giving a sigh like he wished he hadn't said anything.

"What's it done to me?" I repeated, feeling the anger constrict my throat.

He took a deep breath before he spoke. "You take these risks because you've got nothing to lose. You've already accomplished the impossible, so now, there's nothing left. May as well go after the Skull King because it doesn't matter whether you live or die. You've proven to yourself that you aren't worthless, and now that you've done that, you have nothing else to live for. It's as if...you aren't even alive anymore."

It was the same room as last time.

The Royal Suite. Ten thousand euros a night.

I entered the living room and stripped off my jacket along the way. Raindrops had pelted the back window, the sound quiet against the double-paned glass. A couple lamps were on, but for the most part, the room was an array of shadows.

When I walked into the bedroom, I found her waiting for me.

A lamp across the room was lit, so the light hit her subtly where she lay posed on the bed, dressed in a teddy, garter, and black stockings with matching pumps. She reclined, bright lipstick on those plump lips. Hopefully she had more in her purse because all that color would be around my dick in the next few minutes.

My conversation with Benton was forgotten the second I looked at her.

"Goddamn." I yanked my shirt over my head and worked on my jeans. "Get your ass over here."

She obeyed, moving to her knees on the rug, her plump tits pushed together in the lingerie she wore.

I tugged my bottoms down until my cock came free. My hand gripped her neck and my fingers squeezed harder than I should, but she went with it, opening her mouth and flattening her tongue. I shoved my dick inside her mouth, giving her no time to prepare for the assault on her throat.

She gave a muffled gasp, her mouth full of dick.

With my fingers on her neck, I thrust in her mouth, sliding through the saliva that instantly pooled against her cheeks. "Let me show you exactly who you are dealing with, sweetheart." Ruthlessly, I skull-fucked her, barely giving her the opportunity to breathe. I conquered this land like a goddamn conquistador, made sure she would think of me every time someone new shoved his little dick in her mouth.

She not only handled the savagery—she loved it. With saliva dripping down her chin and red cheeks, she could barely contain my pounding dick, but she seemed to love it all the same because her eyes were locked on mine—begging for more.

"Here it comes…" I slowed down my pumps and held her steady as I found my release, coming right on her tongue. Watching her taste my load and swallow it only heightened the euphoria that sent waves of pleasure down my spine. "Show me."

Her makeup was fucked up now. The tears had streaked her mascara and eyeliner. Her lipstick was all over my dick. But she looked better—in my opinion. She stuck out her tongue for me, showing me that she'd swallowed it all.

My dick was still hard like nothing had happened. I wasn't surprised the first or second time we were together because I had been that hard up. But now, it kept going, like those other nights were just warm-ups.

I untied my boots and kicked them away as she got into position on the bed. She lay on her back, her body propped up on her elbows, looking at me as she waited. I finally got my jeans all the way off then crawled up her body, my narrow hips fitting between her soft thighs. I gathered her legs and folded her underneath me, sinking inside her tightness and giving a moan in pleasure. "Fuck, sweetheart... I missed you."

I was propped against the headboard with her sexy thighs straddling my hips. With her hands gripping my shoulders, she rocked her hips and ground against me, pressing her clit against my pelvis, rubbing her ass on my balls.

She came over and over again, her eyes locked on mine, using me as a goddamn sex toy.

What an honor.

Her head rolled back as she finished another round, her palms sliding through the sweat on my chest. Her nails were manicured—painted maroon—and they scratched my skin and made the salt burn the wound. When she finished, she looked at me again, her sexy body shiny with perspiration. "You can come now."

I'd had to wait and watch her get off over and over, unable to join her until she gave her permission.

Fuck...this woman.

I learned I had the restraint of a monk to have my hard dick ridden by the wettest pussy I'd ever known, again and again, and all I could do was sit there and breathe through the pain. Yes, pain.

She rocked into me again, grinding her hips, gripping her tits in my face.

It didn't take much for me to come. Just her permission was all it took. I released, letting my come mix with hers. The climax was so intense after edging myself for so long, letting her get off time and time again.

It felt damn good.

I relaxed against the headboard and closed my eyes briefly. Once the sex was over, I was suddenly aware of how hot I was, how sweaty my skin was. We broke apart, her taking a spot beside me while I headed into the bathroom and took a cold shower.

I was rubbing the bar of soap across my body when the door opened and she joined me, her hair in a high bun to stay dry. She dipped her head back and let the water run over her face, washing away the rivers of makeup.

As I rubbed the bar of soap across my chest, I watched her rinse, seeing the sweat disappear and goose bumps form. Her tits tightened, and her nipples hardened from the cold. She pulled away from the water and squirted body wash into her hand before she scrubbed away all the makeup.

Her eyes didn't pop. Her skin had faded marks from old acne scars. Her lips didn't look as plump without their usual color. But her jawline was still elegant, her neck slender and fair, her eyelashes thick. Unlike most women, she didn't need makeup to be beautiful. It simply enhanced what she already had.

When she felt my stare, she looked at me.

I held up the bar of soap. "May I?"

Those soft lips rose in a slight smile.

I turned the handle to make the water warm so she would be comfortable, even though I still felt the heat scorch my skin. My hand guided the bar across the back of her shoulders, down her spine, and then around her stomach. Once everything was soapy, I gripped her tits in both hands and massaged them with her back to my chest.

"I don't think those are dirty," she said.

I bent my neck down so I could catch her lips. "They feel filthy to me." I kissed her in the shower, her small body coated in the soap my hands had created. My arms kept her close to me, the water pouring down on us both. It got in her hair and soaked it, but she didn't seem to care.

My hand slid down her stomach, and my fingers landed on the button that made her sing. She pushed back lightly into my hand, like even after the hours we'd spent together, she could keep going.

Keep going forever.

I answered the door. "You can set up everything at the dining table."

"Of course, sir." The waiter from room service pushed his cart into the dining room and set up our dinner. A bottle of wine for the table along with a large pitcher of water. Our two entrees with a silver dome on top to keep the food warm. And a basket of bread and butter in the center, not that I would touch it.

I signed the receipt and slipped the cash inside before he left the room.

The second the door clicked closed, Laura appeared, wrapped in a white robe she'd found in the closet. "Is he gone?"

"Yes."

"Good. I'm starving."

My phone had lit up with twenty calls and countless text messages, but nothing seemed urgent, so I ignored it.

She took a seat at the table and removed the lid to her dish. "This looks good."

In just my boxers, I sat across from her and looked at my meal. It was a steak with a side of greens and mashed potatoes.

She smeared butter on her bread and dug into the pasta dish she ordered. Her hair was dry and combed after she'd used the hair dryer in the bathroom, and the way her hair framed her face was hypnotizing for some inexplicable reason.

She caught my stare again and met it.

I didn't look away.

She held the stare for a few moments, but then she looked down at her food again. "Haven't heard from you in a while."

I dropped the linen in my lap and grabbed the utensils. "Busy with work."

"I can imagine."

"I used to have an equal, but he left a few years ago."

"An equal?"

"Another me, basically. Since there's too much work for one single person."

"Why did he leave?"

"Had a kid. Knocked up some woman he couldn't stand."

"Sounds like a happy story…"

If only she knew. "Things are better now. He's married with another on the way."

"And the mother?"

"She bailed," I said. "Which is just as well, because she hated being a mom."

She ate her dinner, sliding a piece of bread through the sauce. "I'm guessing this man is your one friend?"

"Yes."

"So, you guys still talk?"

"We were estranged for years," I said. "Until he asked me to help find his daughter."

"And did you?" she asked.

"Yes."

"It's a good thing he had you to help."

I didn't tell her I was the reason she was taken in the first place. She didn't need to know what kind of monster I was, not for a superficial relationship like this. "I've been looking for his replacement for a long time, but there's no one I trust."

"That sounds lonely."

I gave a shrug. "That leaves a bigger cut for me."

"What's another million when you already have a billion?"

I knew she came from money, so she'd turned her back on luxury for a life of mediocrity. She was one of the few people who could actually put her money where her mouth was. "If you missed me, why didn't you tell me?"

"Who said I missed you?"

"You said you hadn't heard from me in a while. That means you were keeping track of my absence."

"I was just making conversation."

My eyes homed in on her face. "Don't bullshit me."

She went still at my callousness.

"You only seem to like me when we're fucking. The second we're done, you're back to your judgmental stares and icy comments. Be real with me, the way we are in bed, or this is over." I wouldn't be with a woman with two sides. I wouldn't be with a woman who made me feel good when we fucked then made me feel like shit after. "I understand you don't approve of my profession, but forcing yourself to hate me won't make you feel better in the end. You made a choice—now deal with it."

She stopped eating altogether, my words getting deep under her skin. "I know you're busy…and I don't want to bother you." There was no apology, and there would never be an apology. She was far too stubborn for that. But this was good enough—the way she caved because she didn't want to lose me.

She didn't hate me at all. She hated that she *didn't* hate me. "I may be busy, but you could never bother me."

Silence passed, heavy like a cloud of smoke. It hung in the middle of the table between us. We both breathed it in, inhaling toxic fumes that ripped apart our insides. When it became too much, she picked up her fork and began to eat again.

I did the same. "When was your last serious relationship?"

"Why do you assume I ever had one?"

"Because, look at you." Dark hair. Sexy hips perfect for bearing children. Intelligent eyes. If I were a different kind of guy, I'd want her for myself.

"I said we don't have to do pillow talk."

My eyes narrowed. "You're shutting me out."

"Just because we're fucking doesn't mean you're entitled to more of me."

"There's no chance I'll hurt you, so what's the harm?"

She grabbed the stem of her glass and pulled it close. "This is a two-way street, Bartholomew. If you expect me to answer your questions, you have to answer mine."

"I have no issue with that."

Her eyes looked disappointed, like she'd hoped that would be enough to deter me. "My last serious relationship was seven years ago."

Quite the coincidence. "That's a long time to be single."

"I've become disillusioned by love…"

"Did he cheat?" I knew that wasn't it, because what kind of man would fuck around on a woman like this?

"No." She didn't supply an answer, so I knew I wouldn't get one.

"How long was the relationship?"

"Two years."

"I'm happy with this arrangement, but you shouldn't let an asshole from seven years ago sabotage your love life."

She gave a small smile and took a drink.

Now I'd give anything to know what happened. "I could kill him for you—if you want."

She took her drink and set the glass aside. "My ex-husband isn't worth our time."

There was a sudden tightness in my core. It gripped me right in the center of my chest so it was hard to breathe. I kept a stoic expression, but inside, I was struggling with the surprise. "You're divorced."

"Happily divorced." She finished her glass of wine then licked her lips.

"That's awfully young to be married." She would have had to have been in her very early twenties.

"You can thank my father for that."

An arranged marriage.

It was like she could see my thoughts right on my face. "Told you he was an asshole."

9

LAURA

I didn't hear from Bartholomew for days.

We never had back-to-back nights. He left me so sore that an instant replay would probably just hurt. We both filled up our tanks until they were topped off, and then we lived our lives until we started to approach empty.

But as time went on, I drained to empty quicker and quicker. I needed that hit sooner. Needed that man's sweat on my skin, needed the high that only he could give. When the craving became too deep, I sent him a text. *Have plans tonight?*

His message was instantaneous. *Depends on if you're free.*

I am.

Then I have no plans.

Every time I read his messages, I heard his voice in my head. That made me want him more. His confidence. His no-bullshit, no-nonsense attitude. He was the kind of man I liked, with simple desires and straightforward words.

I'll swing by your apartment.

My desire suddenly disappeared. *I don't ever want you here. Made that clear.*

Now his message wasn't instantaneous. Took him a while to respond. *I don't like it when you head home alone in the middle of the night.*

I'm a big girl, Bartholomew.

He didn't say anything.

I'll meet you at our usual place.

When I entered the hotel room, he was already there, his boots next to the armchair where he sat. His jacket was tossed over one of the couches, and he sat there as he enjoyed his tumbler of scotch alone, looking out at the city lights.

I hung my coat on the rack along with my purse then joined him in the living room.

He rose to his feet and headed for me. It seemed like he drew close to speak to me, but his hand slid into my hair and his kiss was on my lips. It all happened fast, and instead of a slow kiss that started at my neck and jawline, he went straight for the kill. His hand was on my ass, and then he lifted me, bringing my legs around his waist as he carried me to the bed.

He tugged off my clothes then fucked me savagely. His hand gripped my neck, squeezing it just enough to make my heart race but not enough to cut off my air supply. With his cheek to mine, he said, "Fuck, sweetheart. Did this pussy get tighter?"

My arms clung to his hard body, my nails digging a little deeper into his flesh. "I think your dick just got bigger…"

His face moved back to mine, his maniacal eyes glued to my face. He took me harder, squeezing my neck tighter than he did before, pounding me so deep into the bed he nearly broke the frame.

Then we came together, a cosmic explosion of two galaxies. Heat from the sun seared us both. Swept away in the euphoria, we moaned in pleasure, grabbing on to each other like we might fly apart if we didn't hold on.

Then it passed, both of us panting, eyes still locked on each other.

"About time you missed me," he said.

Five days had come and gone, and I hadn't heard from him once. The longer my screen remained black, the more disappointed I became. But now I knew it was just a power move. "You were waiting for me?"

"This is a two-way street," he said. "Just remember that."

We developed a routine.

After several rounds of fucking, we showered together then ordered room service. We couldn't dine out together in public, so we shared a meal at our dining table in the Royal Suite. Tonight, he ordered chicken, and I had a Caesar salad with salmon on top.

The meal was spent mostly in silence, the two of us exchanging looks across the table.

"My turn," I said after I took a drink of my wine.

Bartholomew relaxed in the chair, his arms going to the wooden armrests. "I love it when you're on top." He grabbed his glass of wine and flashed me a subtle look of amusement.

He knew exactly what my intention was—and that wasn't it. "When was your last serious relationship?"

He continued his stare, still somewhat amused.

"Two-way street, right?"

A small smile moved on to his handsome face. "Ten years ago."

I could tell he was older than me, but I wasn't sure by how much. Maybe early thirties? So the last time he had a serious woman in his life, he was barely a man. A part of me expected him to say there had never been anyone special. "Were you married?"

"I wanted to be."

I was not expecting that answer. And I couldn't hide my reaction, the way my eyes widened a bit. I assumed Bartholomew was one of those guys who couldn't feel anything more than lust. "What happened?"

He tilted his head slightly. "You really want to know?"

If he answered my question, I'd be obligated to answer his. I didn't want to share this information with him, not with anyone, but I was so interested in his story that I couldn't pass up the opportunity. "Yes."

He stared for a moment. "Alright." He sank into the chair, his elbow propped and his curled fingers underneath his chin. "Her name was Nina. Met at a bar. Was supposed to be a one-time thing, but…that didn't happen. This was long before my time as a drug kingpin, so I was a regular guy, just trying to make it. I'd been using and she didn't know, so I got clean before she could figure it out."

It was impossible to picture the life he described, so it made the story even more interesting.

"Things got serious. Asked her to move in. But then I met her parents…" Instead of looking hurt by the memory, he grinned as if it were all a joke. "They didn't like me one bit. Saw me for what I was—trash. Nina came from a nice family, two loving parents with a protective older brother. Ran a small restaurant that had been in their family for generations. I was some *kid* with no parents who grew up in an orphanage, with no real future, nothing I could offer her except my heart—which was worthless, apparently."

My eyes stayed on his, but it was hard to keep a straight face and not pity him.

"She dumped me shortly after that meeting."

"I'm sorry."

His eyes shifted away like he hadn't heard me, like he was deep in thought. "She got married a few years afterward. An accountant." He gave a quiet chuckle. "Most boring shit I've ever heard."

Now it all made sense. "That's why you're so ambitious…"

His eyes flicked back to me.

"That's why you've turned yourself into this powerful drug lord," I said. "If only she could see you now…"

Despite the seriousness of the moment, he chose to look amused. "If she could see me now, she would know that her parents were right and she made the right decision. My ambition is driven purely by money and power—not some girl I loved when I was hardly a man."

"How different your life would have been if she'd stayed." Instead of running the streets and killing people who revolted against his oppression, he would be fulfilled by the love of a woman, would be a father, would have in-laws who replaced the love he lost from his parents. For the first time, I actually felt bad for him, seeing past his hard shell to the broken man underneath.

"She did us both a favor. She's where she's supposed to be—and I'm exactly where I belong." He stared at me across the table, the amusement leaving his face. Now the seriousness descended like a dark shadow. "Your turn, sweetheart."

Was his answer worth mine? I was about to find out. "He left me."

His expression didn't change at all, like he expected more. "Why?"

"I'd rather not say."

His eyes flicked back and forth between mine. "Why?"

My heart started to pound. Adrenaline made my insides tight. There had been a draft in the suite a moment ago, but now I felt suffocated by heat. "I don't want you to look at me differently. Because if you do...you'll walk away too."

"Remember who you're talking to, sweetheart." His confident gaze pierced me from across the table. "I'm not the judgmental type. Nothing you say will change my perception of you. And nothing you say will make me want to fuck you less."

When he commanded the room like that, I wanted to believe every word of it, but I couldn't.

"Well, let me take that back. If you fucked a kid or killed a kid…that would leave a bad taste in my mouth. But I know that's not your crime."

He was so far off. "No…not that."

He looked at me expectantly, waiting for the revelation.

"I told you my father is an asshole, and I'm not the only one who thinks so." I couldn't believe I was about to do this. About to reveal the secret I'd never shared with anyone except my ex-husband. "My father pissed off some people…and instead of going after him, they came after my mother and me." I swallowed, feeling the nerves get to me. There were no hot tears in the back of my throat. It had happened so long ago that I'd moved on. But it still felt like I was standing trial at the moment. "They killed her. And then they…came after me." I broke eye contact because I didn't want to see his reaction. Didn't want him to pretend it didn't bother him when it did.

Silence stretched for a long time. All we did was breathe.

Then I finally looked at him again.

His expression was exactly the same. "I already know, sweetheart."

"You do...?"

"Put two and two together a while ago."

I looked away again. "He treated me differently afterward. Wouldn't touch me. Didn't want me anymore. Then he left."

Another stretch of silence ensued.

"I'm sorry that happened to you." He wore a hard expression, but his eyes shone like he meant every word he said. "Are they dead?"

"Who?"

"The men who did this to you."

"I—I don't know." Survival had been my priority at the time. Not revenge.

"Then I'll find out and take care of it."

"That's a bit hypocritical, don't you think?"

His eyes narrowed instantly.

"You're a crime lord. I'm sure your men do the same shit." They were criminals without morals. When someone crossed them, they probably raped their daughters. There was no law—like it was medieval times.

He was silent for a very long time. "We don't. And I'm deeply offended by the accusation." The tension in the room changed. Now it was heavy with his rage, like a fire that started in the corner and slowly engulfed the entire room. Smoke came out of his eyes. Without raising his voice or saying anything else, it felt like he would kill me and everyone else in the hotel.

Then he got to his feet and approached me.

I remained steady.

In just his boxers, he looked at me. "I'm a businessman who sells a product and kills anyone who interferes with my business. *That's it*. I don't seek revenge on my enemies by raping their wives and daughters. I don't punish civilians for being in the wrong place at the wrong time. I won't pretend I'm a good man, far from it, but this is…is a fucking slap in the face."

I cowered beneath him, immediately regretting what I said.

"Just because something happens to you, that doesn't make it who you are. It's a verb, not a noun. It doesn't change the way I feel about you whatsoever. I'd take you on the table right now if I weren't so pissed off." His angry eyes continued to bore into mine. "Apologize when you're ready. And if you don't—take care." With that, he walked away, pulled on his clothes, and left the hotel room.

The next few days passed with aching slowness. I went to the gym every morning, got ready, and then went to work for over twelve hours. I didn't just have to pick out the clothes for my clients, but I also had to alter them. Having a seamstress do it for me was always an option, but every time I tried, their work wasn't good enough. Clothes didn't fit correctly, and these clients weren't paying top dollar for something half-assed. As a result, I had to do everything for the business, and I meant everything.

Once I sat down for more than a couple minutes, my thoughts drifted back to the last conversation I'd had with Bartholomew. Venom had burned in his eyes. It was a harsh thing to say, but I was used to the world that my father had created, a world where any crime was justifiable for crossing him.

Looked like Bartholomew didn't share that sentiment.

I grabbed my phone and fired off a message. *Can we talk?*

His response was immediate. *Took you long enough.* Even though he was busy running a drug empire, he was never too busy to respond to my messages. *I'm out right now. I'll swing by later.*

I already told you how I feel about that.

No one is tailing me, and if they were, they would already know all about you. Just because we meet at a hotel doesn't mean you're invisible. I put up with the whole charade to make you feel better, but it really makes no difference at all.

I read those words more than once and let them sink in.

I'll be there within an hour.

I set my phone on the table and waited.

He opened my front door and let himself in. Dressed for the night, he was in his black bomber jacket, black jeans, and the same boots he always wore. He might as well have tattooed "Bad Boy" right on his forehead.

His eyes found mine as I sat at the small dining table, and he took his time as he crossed the room and approached me. Every time his boots hit the wood, it was a distinct thud, showing his heaviness despite his leanness.

He took a seat across from me, one arm resting on the surface of the table, his hard eyes looking at me with coldness.

I suddenly wondered if he carried a gun, because whenever he undressed in front of me, it was nowhere to be found. Maybe he left it in the car.

He continued to stare, waiting for the apology that was long overdue.

"I'm sorry...for what I said."

He remained still, as if he expected more.

"I just know that most men do that sort of thing…"

"*Most men?*" he asked in an incredulous tone. "What kind of men do you keep in your company?"

Perhaps this would make more sense if he knew about my past, where I come from, who my father was…but I kept it to myself. "Are there a lot of lines that criminals won't cross?"

"You're confusing a criminal with an asshole—and there's a big difference. Men like me, the top of the food chain, don't get there by doing whatever we want and causing havoc. Good criminals, the ones who stay alive and get shit done, live by a code of ethics." He started to count off the rules on his fingers. "Keep your word. Spare the police. Dismiss civilians. That's pretty much it."

"Dismiss civilians…?"

"Sometimes people are in the wrong place at the wrong time. They don't deserve to die because of it."

"How do you get them to keep their mouth shut?"

"We don't," he said with a slight shrug. "Most of the police force is on my payroll, so sometimes they'll be dispatched to investigate what we're doing. I let them do what they've got to do...and then they're eventually called off by my guys. No one has to die."

"Why do you spare them?"

He considered my words for a long time. "They're just doing their jobs, right? Looking for a paycheck to support their families and whatnot. Besides, they take care of the little guys on the street, so I don't have to. We're allies—even if they don't know it."

I believed he wasn't pulling my chain, making me believe in some lie.

He sank in the chair, arms crossing over his chest, his head cocked slightly.

"I said I was sorry—"

"But it was immediately followed by a justification for your assumption. You basically said, 'I'm sorry I accused you of something so disgusting, *but* it was a fair assumption because of A and B.'" He continued to stare at me with those angry eyes. "In case you haven't noticed, I get pussy without even asking for it. I definitely don't need to take it by force."

"And if your men were to do that?"

"They definitely aren't doing it on the job. We're too busy working. And we have a running tab with the brothels, so they can get their jollies there."

"Is that what you do?" I asked point-blank.

"Yes." He answered my question without hesitation, without shame. "I pay for sex regularly—except for now, of course."

Now I did feel a bit foolish for assuming he was anything like my father. Never met a drug lord so blatantly honest. "I really am sorry for what I said."

For the first time, the coldness melted off his face, and his body became less rigid. "Thank you."

"You seem like an honest guy."

"Too honest—as I've been told."

We sat there in silence for a while. He stared at me. I stared at him. His quiet rage seemed to evaporate slowly as the minutes ticked by.

"I was just about to make dinner. Would you like to join me?"

He gave a slow nod. "Sounds good, sweetheart."

We'd just finished dinner when he abruptly walked away.

Headed for my bedroom, he stripped off his jacket and left it on the floor. His shirt came next, a breadcrumb trail leading through the open door to my bedroom. He sat on the edge of the bed and unlaced his boots before he yanked them off and unbuttoned his jeans. He stood up and pushed those down before he removed his boxers.

Hard as a rock.

He looked at me across the room. "Get your ass in here, sweetheart." He lay back on the bed, his back supported against the headboard, his fat dick propped up against his stomach.

The glass of wine hovered at my lips for seconds, mesmerized by the naked man now in my bed. I finally drank the red at the bottom of my glass before I entered the bedroom. My heart was always in my throat when it came to him. I experienced this indescribable rush that made me feel numb and also alive. He made me just a little bit nervous, but not nervous enough that I wanted to run away.

At the foot of the bed, I undressed, taking my time removing every piece of clothing as his eyes took me in. When my bra was gone, his eyes were right at my tits, and that hard dick suggested that he wasn't thinking about my confession, that he didn't think about the men who'd come before him, especially those who weren't invited.

I removed everything else, standing there in nothing but my birthday suit.

With his fingers locked behind his head, he looked at me appreciatively. "Now show me how sorry you are."

The baritone of his voice was seductive. The deep look in his eyes had the pull of a magnet. He guided me toward him with his silent command, and after I crawled up the bed and his long body, I parked my sex right on top of his.

His big hands immediately went to my ass, and he kneaded my cheeks as he looked at my tits. He leaned forward and kissed the valley between my tits, playing with my ass as he guided his tongue over my skin. He tasted my nipples, kissed the hollow of my throat, rocked his hips slightly so he could grind against my sex.

His rock-hard length was perfect against my clit, the pressure just right to make my thighs quiver. My arms hooked around his shoulders, and I arched my back as he guided himself inside me. His head pushed past my entrance, and then I sank down his length, my nails clawing deep into him all the way down.

His hand suddenly gave my ass a hard smack. "Fuck, I missed this pussy." He guided me up and down, wanting to take me hard and fast right from the start. With my palms on his shoulders, I rode him at the pace he commanded, that big dick filling me over and over. It was so good. I started to dread when this situationship would be over because no other guy could fuck like this one.

"Say it." He thrust into me from below, his eyes locked on mine with that maniacal gleam.

My hands slid down to his chest, my clit dragging perfectly against his body. I already felt the tension in my stomach, the white-hot heat that was about to burn me from the inside out.

He smacked my ass again, this time hard enough to leave a mark. "*Say it.*"

"I-I'm sorry."

His thumb moved to my clit, and he rubbed it hard, bringing me to a climax on the heels of my apology.

"I'm sorry…" My head rolled back as I felt that unbelievable pleasure between my legs, a goodness that could only be caused by this perfect man. "I'm sorry."

His thumb pulled away from my clit, and then he maneuvered me to my back, his body dominating mine, pressing me into the mattress and covering me with his heat. His dick remained buried inside me the entire time, and his arms pinned my knees back as he folded me underneath him. He fucked me hard and fast. "I forgive you, sweetheart."

"I miss the hotel." I lay on my side and looked at him.

He was on his back, one hand resting on his stomach, the sheets at his waist because he was still warm. There was still a faint sheen to his skin. "Really? I prefer it here."

"That shower was unbelievable. And they had room service..."

He grinned slightly. "We just ate."

"Yeah, but my cooking is no match."

"I prefer yours."

I rolled my eyes. "You already have me, so give it a rest."

"Not pulling your chain."

"That view..."

"You got me there." He turned to look at me fully. "But this is the only view I care about."

It was just a line, but he looked so handsome as he said it that I felt warm inside. "You're smooth."

"Guess I'm a natural." He looked at the ceiling again, his dark hair messy from the way I'd played with it. "As much as I'd like to stay, the night is young."

"You're like a vampire."

He gave a slight smirk. "I'd definitely feed on you if I were." He left the bed and stood up, his chiseled body fine in the limited light. He had a tight ass, a sculpted back, and a bunch of veins all over his arms. He started to get dressed, covering his beautiful body with his clothes.

I wanted him to stay—but I'd never ask.

I got out of bed and tied my robe around my body.

He stilled as he looked at me, clearly thinking about the first time he'd come over and I was dressed in nothing but the black lace. Consternation spread across his handsome face, and it seemed like he might change his mind and stay.

But he didn't.

I walked him to the door, his heavy boots thudding against the hardwood floor.

"I gotta ask."

He turned to me, his chin dipped to look down at me.

"What's with the boots?"

He cocked his head slightly, letting the silence linger as he regarded me with those earth-colored eyes.

"I mean, they're combat boots."

"You really want to know why?" He challenged me, his eyes flicking back and forth between mine.

Now I wasn't sure.

He kneeled and pulled out a four-inch knife stashed away in a single compartment. He turned it over in his hand, showing its razor-sharp edge. "That's not all." He kneeled again and quickly removed the lace from his boots. He stood upright again, tightening the strands around both of his wrists, and then he hooked the lace behind my neck and tugged me close so he could kiss me. "That's why." He let me go then re-laced his boots quickly, like he'd done it a hundred times. The knife was stowed away, and he was back on his feet. "Good night, sweetheart." He stepped into the hallway.

"Bartholomew?"

He halted then slowly turned to regard me again. He always had a straight posture, his broad shoulders back, his eyes intense. Patiently, he waited for me to speak, even though the underworld required his attention.

"Thanks for…not treating me differently." He showed his sympathy, but he didn't treat me like a victim. Instead of acting like I was damaged goods or irreparable, he carried on as if it were nothing more than a scratch on my knee. The ordeal was a traumatizing experience, but the way my husband treated me afterward was far more traumatizing. He was the one who made me feel…dirty.

Bartholomew stared at me for a while, like it took him a moment to even understand what I was thanking him for. "Your ex is just as bad as the men who did that to you. I thought about killing him too—but I knew you would say no."

"You're really going to kill them?"

"Did you think it was a joke?"

"No. I just… It's not your problem."

"Not my problem?" His voice turned cold. "For as long as this lasts, I'm your man. So, yes, it is my goddamn problem. I will kill every one of them, and before I do, they'll be begging me to finish the job."

I almost felt bad for them. "What if they have families—"

"I don't care. I will stomp on their heads until their skulls shatter and their brains are all over the floor. Then I'll do the next one—and then the next. Oh, and that's another reason I wear these…just didn't think you'd want to know that."

"What's the occasion?" I stood at the counter as I spoke to a client on the phone.

"Another one of those charity galas..."

"What's the charity for?"

"I don't know," she said. "Some kind of disease or something... I'm only interested in finding a new husband. You know, since mine chose to run off with his secretary."

"So, you need to look hot. Got it."

"Exactly."

"Alright, I'll work my magic." I set down the phone and flipped through my notes, looking through her measurements to decide what kind of style would best show off her assets. I went to all the fashion shows. Had all the magazine subscriptions. Did everything I could to stay on top of the hottest trends.

My phone started to ring.

I assumed it was another client, so my hand moved quicker than my mind. I took the call before I could truly process who was on the other end.

My father.

But now, it was too late. He was on the line.

I stared at the screen for several seconds before I brought the phone to my ear.

"Didn't expect you to answer." His voice was exactly the same as I remembered, masculine and full of arrogance. It'd aged a bit, which was no surprise because it'd been almost a decade since we'd last spoken.

"Thought you were someone else."

He processed the insult in silence.

"Are you calling for a reason?" Most of the time, I didn't think about my father at all. But there were times when the estrangement was painful, especially during the holidays that I spent alone or with friends. But he'd made his decision—and I made mine.

"Uncle Tony passed away."

When someone passed away, they had a heart attack or lost their battle with cancer. They went in their sleep or died instantly in a brutal car wreck. Things that were out of their control. But I knew none of those circumstances applied to Uncle Tony. "I'm sorry to hear that."

"He was a good brother."

Because he blindly followed your orders—and got killed for it. "Thanks for letting me know."

"Funeral's on Friday—if you can make it."

Florence had been my home my entire life. The Duomo was the first thing I saw out the bedroom window every morning. I'd walked those narrow streets eating pistachio gelato with friends. I'd gone out to explore the city at two in the morning and never felt afraid. I still missed it… always would.

"Laura?"

"I—I have to think about it."

"You always seemed fond of him."

He was a better father than you were at times. "I was."

"Then pay your respects."

"Don't tell me what to do, Leonardo." Now we were on a first-name basis. I hadn't called him Father in nearly a decade, even though I referred to him that way in my mind or when I mentioned him to anyone who asked about him. It was a sign of disrespect, a reminder that I still hated him with every fiber of my being.

His temper seemed to have improved, because he took the blow in silence. "I'd also like to see you. It's been a long time since I last saw your face."

The feeling wasn't mutual.

When my father knew he wouldn't get anything else out of me, he let me go. "Hope to see you there."

10

BARTHOLOMEW

I left my bedroom in my sweatpants, the curtains open to let the sunshine into the top floor of the apartment. It was hard to tell what time of day it was just by looking outside, but it was probably sometime after three o'clock.

My butler already had the table set, an Americano with steak and scrambled egg whites with whatever organic produce he'd found at the market earlier that morning. The newspaper was there, even though I hardly ever read it. I took a seat, rubbed the sleep from my eyes, and then sorted through all the texts, emails, and calls that had exploded my phone throughout the morning.

My butler didn't speak to me—which was how I preferred to spend my mornings.

Or, should I say, afternoons.

My peaceful silence was interrupted when my butler approached the table. "Bleu is here to see you, sir. Shall I let him in?"

My eyes lifted from my newspaper and steadied on his face. Call me old-fashioned, but I didn't like to start my mornings with bullshit, though I assumed it was important. "Yes."

He ushered Bleu inside a moment later, and he sat across from me at the table as I cut into my steak. "I figured it out with the Moroccans. They'll agree to be our exclusive distributor—for a hefty price."

"I don't care what the price is."

"They just put a supply on the cargo ship, so that delivery can't be reversed. After that, they'll cut them off. So, we have two weeks."

"Good." I chewed a large bite, loving the taste of steak with coffee.

Bleu sat there across from me, looking out the window like he thought it was rude to watch me eat. "Still think this is a good idea?"

"Absolutely."

"What will you do once the Skull King knows his supply is being cut off?"

"Ask him to sell my drugs instead."

"And you don't think he'll figure all this out?"

I shrugged as I cut into my steak. "It doesn't matter if he does. He has no choice. Either work for me or go out of business. That simple."

I sat in the bar, talking shop with one of my distributors. The night was young. While people had their dinner, I hadn't even had lunch yet. We smoked cigars and drank, talking about the millions of pounds we moved through France and out of Eastern Europe that week.

"Our infiltration into Croatia has been very successful. Our product is also superior to what Roan had before, so we've managed to increase the market price." He drank his scotch until the glass was empty, and he left it on the table.

"Maybe we should move through Germany and then Russia."

He gave a quiet chuckle. "You're crazy, you know that?"

"Am I?" I asked, releasing the smoke from my mouth. "Or am I the only one thinking clearly?"

"Russia is a whole different ball game. Mean motherfuckers."

I gave a shrug. "We'll see."

A woman caught his attention at the bar, inviting him over with a wave and a smile. Seemed like they already knew each other.

"If we're done here, I'd like to get my dick wet."

I raised my glass and clinked it against his. "Go for it."

He left me sitting there alone, and I finished the rest of my glass before I opened my wallet and threw the bills on the table.

A hand gripped me by the shoulder. Long nails dug through my jacket, the touch possessive like this wasn't the first time she'd touched me. Then her legs came into my view in that short dress, and she helped herself onto one of my knees like I was fucking Santa Claus. Her arm hooked around my shoulder, and she looked down at me. "Long time, no see."

"I'm a hard man to pin down."

She took the cigar out of my hand and took a puff. She tried to be sexy, but then she had to cough a little because she couldn't pull it off. She dropped it into the ashtray. "Want to get out of here?"

"As tempting as that is, Chloe…I have somewhere to be."

"But you're the big boss man, right?" she asked. "You don't have to be anywhere you don't want to be."

I started to stand up, forcing her to get off my knee and balance on her heels. "True. But I've made a commitment to someone—and I keep my commitments."

She narrowed her eyes as she studied me, trying to solve a puzzle without any hints. "What kind of commitment are we talking here?"

"Monogamy."

Both of her eyebrows moved up her face. "Bartholomew is committed to one woman and only one woman?"

"My dick is, at least." I started to walk away. "Have a good night, Chloe."

Want to stop by?

Just reading that message made me hard. I had a hot little woman sit in my lap in the bar and I felt nothing, but reading Laura's words was like foreplay. *Damn right I do.* I had a couple things on the schedule tonight, but I delegated them to Bleu and others so I could swing by her apartment and make her come.

When I reached her apartment, I let myself inside because I knew the door would be unlocked. She sat at the small dining table, enjoying a bottle of wine by herself. She was in the same little black robe she'd worn before, and she made that piece of fabric sexier than the skimpiest lingerie.

I took the seat across from her and poured myself a glass. I preferred the stronger stuff like gin and scotch, but I'd come to appreciate the palate of a wine drinker. All those subtle differences in the harvest, of the bold reds and the sweet whites. It was a little fancy for my taste, but being a billionaire had inadvertently made me a little fancy.

As I studied her face, I noticed the small changes, differences that her closest friends probably wouldn't notice. Her skin was a little fairer, her eyes were more guarded but also more vulnerable at the same time. While she was dressed for business, her mind seemed elsewhere.

She wanted me here for a different reason.

So she could talk about her problems.

And I could listen.

That was not what I'd signed up for. I came to fuck—not to play therapist. But instead of being an asshole like I always was, I patiently waited for her to start. A part of me was curious what had brought her down, because she was as still as a mountain when she told me what happened to her seven years ago. "What is it, sweetheart?" I couldn't be patient any longer, needing to know what would faze a woman like her.

Her eyes lifted to mine, her fingers still on her glass. "My uncle died."

I gave a slow nod. "I'm sorry."

"Don't be." She took a drink. "It's his own fault."

"Drunk driving?"

"Being a crony of my father's."

Now I gave another nod. "I see." Another reason she wanted nothing to do with that life, and now I wondered how this conversation would end. Would it be another reminder that sleeping with me was a bad idea? I hoped not—even though she was right on the money. "Were you close to him?"

"I used to be."

"Have you spoken to him since you left?"

"Called me on my birthday every year. We never talked about anything real, just the weather and French cuisine...shit like that."

I loved the way she sounded when she cursed. Like she didn't give a damn about anything or anyone. "He was your father's brother?"

"Yes. Losing his wife wasn't enough..."

"And his daughter."

She grabbed her glass and took a drink. "I've decided to go to the funeral. I'm leaving tomorrow."

I was a master at keeping a straight face, and that ability didn't fail me now, so she had no idea that my stomach just dropped. Their estrangement made her useless to me, but if they stopped being estranged...it might get messy. "Why?"

"My uncle deserves to have someone there who actually cared about him."

"And what will you do about your father?" A funeral was already a miserable affair. Throw in an uncomfortable reunion and that place would turn into a furnace of tension.

She took a long drink of her wine. "No idea."

"Was he the one who called you?"

"Yes."

"And how was that?"

"Brief. Cold. *Blah*." She drank her wine again, and now her glass was empty. "But enough about that. That's not what you came here for."

Not at all. But now, it was all I could think about. How could a man have a daughter like her and let her walk away? How could he not bust his ass every day to make it right? How could he have let anything happen to her in the first place? I wasn't one to judge, but he should have put his family before his work, and the fact that he didn't told me everything I needed to know about his character. "I'll come with you."

She pulled the tie cinched at her waist so the robe slightly came apart, opening across her chest to reveal more of those perky tits. Succulent skin. Unblemished by my aggressive kiss. If it opened just a little more, her nipples would be exposed. "Come with me where?" She ran her fingers through her thick hair next, pulling it from her face and exposing more of her neck.

"Florence."

She stilled when she understood the offer. "What?"

"You could use the company. I have business there anyway."

"What business?"

I took a drink of my wine. When the silence continued, the realization sank into her bones—that I wouldn't answer.

"I don't want you near my family."

I did my best not to smirk at the irony. "I didn't invite myself to the funeral, just your bed. We could stay at my place in Florence. You do your business, and I do mine. And if you need a shoulder to cry on...you can have mine."

"This is supposed to be a clandestine affair...and now we're taking trips together?"

"Not how I would describe it." My eyes remained on her face, but they were tempted to look down, to pray that the robe would slip a little more...and a little more. I hadn't tit-fucked a woman since I was a teenager, but I could definitely see myself sliding between those plump tits. "We could take my plane. Private is the only way to travel."

"And you aren't going to tell me what you're doing there?"

"Do you really want to know, sweetheart?" There were nights when I left her at the hotel and went straight to the docks to execute traitors and stuff them in oil barrels before they were dumped by cargo ships somewhere in the Atlantic on their way to their next destination. She didn't need to know about my barbarism.

She seemed to agree because she dropped the subject. "Alright." Her fingers slid down the sides of her robe before she pulled it off, letting the silk material leave her petite shoulders and crumple in the chair behind her. Silky-smooth skin was exposed, her nipples immediately hardening once they felt the cold air directly.

I'd considered myself to be an ass man, but not anymore.

She rose from the chair and walked right past me toward the bedroom. In nothing but a tiny little thong that hardly covered anything, she moved across the room, all woman with those sexy hips and those toned thighs, that nectarine ass I could see myself fucking at some point.

As if I were paralyzed, all I could do was watch her enter the bedroom and hook her thumbs into her panties. Then she bent over, pushing the panties down to her ankles, enticing me with a very provocative view.

Like I didn't already want to fuck her brains out.

Then she looked at me over her shoulder, her eyes so commanding they burned straight into me.

I think that was the biggest turn-on of all.

I lay beside her, most of her naked body exposed above the sheets because she was still warm, even though I was the one who'd done all the work tonight.

No complaints.

She was the kind of woman that made me want to do all the dirty work—no pun intended. Her eyes opened like she knew I was staring at her, and she looked at me. She was on her side, her face close to my shoulder. She held my look for a while but didn't say anything.

I appreciated her confidence. When she made eye contact, she wasn't in a hurry to look away and pretend it never happened. She could hold her own against me, never become dwarfed by my intensity. I was very aware of the way I made people around me feel, either intimidated or outright scared.

That didn't apply to Laura.

"It's time for me to go." A full night awaited my attention. My men knew I wasn't as focused as I normally was, that I showed up late to meetings or didn't come at all. But no one dared question me about it.

"Is this how it'll be in Florence?" she asked. "Will you be gone all night?"

"Maybe."

"You're like a vampire. Sleep all day…out all night."

"It's fitting—because I spill a lot of blood."

Growing up in an Italian crime family must have made her numb to these sorts of things, because she didn't give any reaction. She'd initially wanted nothing to do with me because of my criminal behavior, but now she excused all of it because I made her come so hard. "What time do you want to leave tomorrow?"

"Late afternoon." After I woke up.

"Alright. I'll be ready." She left the bed and pulled on a large t-shirt, a t-shirt that fit her like a blanket. It was gray with a V neck. I wasn't into fashion, but as a man, I could tell it was a man's shirt—and it wasn't mine.

A bolt of lightning flashed through me. The heat was searing on my extremities. Even made my eyes burn. I suddenly felt hot everywhere, the same heat before I exploded and killed someone with my boot.

But then I swallowed—and it passed.

I got out of bed and put on my clothes. Slipped on my boots before I tied them tight. She walked me to the door, her hair disheveled from the fucking, her lips a little plumper from all the kissing. Her makeup was now ruined, the tears she'd shed streaking everything below her eyes.

But all I could think about was that shirt.

That fucking shirt.

She opened the door, not caring if someone happened to be in the hallway and caught a glimpse of her half naked.

"Good night." Her hand remained on the handle, and she watched me cross the threshold.

We never kissed each other good night or embraced. All she did was let me out. "Good night." I moved into the hallway and heard the door shut behind me. The lock clicked a moment later.

But then I halted.

Let it go.

I stood there, looking at the stairs at the very end, willing myself to move forward.

Let. It. Go.

I clenched my jaw, feeling anger I couldn't control. It was like riding a wild horse without reins.

I turned back around.

Fuck.

I knocked on her door and waited.

It took her a moment to come back to the door, and when she did, her hair was in a bun, like she was about to brush her teeth and wash her face before bed. "Did you forget something?"

"No."

Her eyes shifted back and forth between mine before she backed away slightly. "Is there a problem...?"

I invited myself inside and shut the door. "Yes." I stared down at her, watching her cross her arms over her chest and hug that shirt even closer to her body.

"Are you going to tell me what it is—"

"Whose shirt is that?"

She paused for a second before she looked down at what she wore. It took her several seconds to catch up to me, to understand what got me hotter than a volcano. "It's just a shirt—"

"Answer my question." Sometimes my temper got the best of me and I acted like the psychotic drug lord that I was, but I had to restrain my voice, keep my body absolutely still. Otherwise, I would scare her off.

Her arms crossed over her chest again, like she didn't want to answer the question. "It doesn't matter—"

"Why won't you answer my fucking question?" I still didn't yell, but I seethed—hard.

"Because it's none of your business," she snapped. "That's why."

I stopped breathing for a moment, so pissed off with her lack of compliance that I wanted to smash all the wooden chairs around her dining table. "None of my business?" I took a step toward her, and instinctively, she took a step back. "If you came to my home and found a thong in my top drawer, you'd be asking the same question."

"I would not—"

"Don't fuck with me right now." Now the anger emerged, hot through my clenched jaw, loud in the tone of my voice. "*Answer. Me.*"

Her arms loosened, letting the material release from her waist. I couldn't tell if she was scared of how angry I was or scared that she would lose me if she didn't cooperate, but she finally gave me what I wanted. "Some guy left it over here a long time ago. It's a really nice shirt, and I like to wear it to bed. That's all."

The monster inside me continued to rear its ugly head. It came out of nowhere, a beast I didn't even know I had. "You want a nice shirt?" I yanked off my jacket and let it drop to the floor with a thud. Then I stripped off my black t-shirt before I placed it against her chest. "Here you go."

She grabbed the shirt, her eyes still on me.

I put the jacket back on and zipped it up to hide my nakedness underneath.

She continued to grip the shirt, still astonished by the way this night had unfolded.

I walked out the door, and this time, I didn't say good night.

11

LAURA

After I finished up at the office, I packed up my things for the trip.

A knock sounded on the door just when I finished.

My heart skipped a beat because I knew who it was. I'd never seen him that angry before. The way his jaw was so tight. The way his arms trembled slightly as if he couldn't contain his rage. The scariest part was the way he worked so hard to restrain himself. It gave me a glimpse into the man he was on the streets.

I was lucky I got the watered-down version. "It's open."

Heavy boots thudded against the floor, and that was how I knew it was Bartholomew.

"I'll be right there." I grabbed my suitcase and my bag, along with my purse that held my passport and cash. I entered the main living area, seeing him in a black t-shirt and jeans. It was a warm day for spring, so his signature jacket was gone, but not his coldness.

Yep. He was still pissed. "You don't have to come."

"Did I say I didn't want to come?"

"Well, you look like you're about to scream at me."

"I always look like that."

"Trust me, you don't." There was his intense stare that made me feel like his property even when he didn't touch me. And then there was this look…like he wanted to strangle me. "How long are you going to be angry?"

"Until you apologize."

"Apologize?" I asked incredulously. "I didn't do anything wrong—"

"You disrespected me."

"Disrespected you? You aren't my boyfriend, Bartholomew—"

"I'm your man. We established this already."

I set my purse on the floor because this conversation just got real. "We're fucking. That's it. Don't you dare make this into a relationship, because that's the last thing I want—"

"I said nothing about a relationship. But as long as I'm the man you're sleeping with, you're mine. As long as I'm faithful to you, then I'm yours. That means I respect you and you respect me. Wearing another man's shirt to bed right after I fucked you all night is a goddamn slap in the face." He stepped closer to me. "Do I look like a man who gets slapped in the face?"

I held my ground and didn't step back, but it was hard not to. My heart was beating so fast it was like a speeding train. I wasn't sure if I was terrified, nervous, or even aroused. Maybe it was all of the above.

"Answer me."

"No," I said quickly.

"Then apologize."

I held his gaze, refusing to cave.

"*Now.*"

"No."

He cocked his head slightly, his eyes angry. "Apologize, or I walk away."

Shit.

He waited, standing over me like a skyscraper.

I didn't want to cave. Didn't want to admit defeat. But I knew he didn't make idle threats—and I couldn't lose this man. "I'm sorry." I said it so quietly that both of us could barely hear it.

"On your knees."

"*Excuse me—*"

"Get on your knees and apologize to me."

"You're a fucking asshole—"

"Yes, I know," he said. "Now, do it."

A silent standoff ensued. He stared hard. I stared back.

He wouldn't give me ground. Not an inch. Not a goddamn centimeter.

With pure self-loathing, I lowered myself to the floor.

His eyes intensified as he relished his victory.

"I'm sorry." *There. Done.*

His hands moved for the top of his jeans. He popped the button. Pulled down the fly. And then got his big dick in his hand before he grabbed me by the neck. "Now show me how sorry you are."

The moment my lips parted, he rubbed his dick around my mouth, like he was giving me a coat of lipstick.

My mouth opened farther and my tongue flattened, so he could enter me.

He invited himself inside, pushing his whole dick in and leaving it there, not letting me breathe, his fingers gripping my neck possessively. "Say it."

With a mouth full of dick, I said the words. "I'm sorry." It came out as an incoherent mumble, saliva spilling from the corners of my mouth. That dick was so good in my mouth that I spent the next ten minutes sucking it as hard as I could, getting spit everywhere, ruining the makeup I'd spent thirty minutes applying, ignoring the pain in my knees as I kneeled directly on the hardwood floor, proving just how fucking sorry I really was.

He gave a loud groan of satisfaction as he came in my mouth, his hand supporting the back of my neck as he finished, his handsome face tinted red, his look far more possessive than it'd ever been before. "Good job, sweetheart. You've earned my forgiveness."

We used to travel by private plane when I was growing up, so it wasn't that much of a surprise. But Bartholomew's plane was still very luxurious, and the second I took a seat, I remembered how much I missed the lifestyle. Champagne. Caviar. Assorted French cheeses. We didn't have to go through security. We didn't have to wait for our luggage to be loaded. We didn't have to wait on the tarmac. We just pulled up and took off.

Bartholomew was on his computer the entire time, not paying attention to me during the flight. His flight attendants were all over him, like they lived for the opportunity to serve him. I imagined that carried over to all women in his life.

They'd love to beg for his forgiveness the way I just did.

I continued to sip my champagne, but the alcohol couldn't cleanse his taste from my tongue—not that I wanted it to.

A while later, we landed in Florence, the Duomo visible from the air before we made our landing. It was a beautiful day, all sunshine and no clouds, and the instant my feet were on the ground, I felt the comfort of home.

A black SUV picked us up, and when there was no conversation, I assumed the driver was on Bartholomew's payroll. It was a short drive to the heart of the city, the roads flooded with cars and motorbikes. We passed the Four Seasons then pulled up to a palace with a private gate.

Once the doors were shut, our luggage was unloaded, and Bartholomew was greeted by a man in a tuxedo—probably the butler for the residence.

"I hope you had a good flight, sir." He acknowledged Bartholomew with a slight bow. "The residence is prepared for your arrival. I'll be in the parlor if you need anything."

Bartholomew gave a nod before he entered the house.

The butler approached me next and gave me the same level of respect. "I'm Henry, the butler of Bartholomew's Florence residence. Please let me know if you need anything, and I'll be happy to assist you."

We used to have a butler growing up. It was the best. "Thank you, Henry."

We were escorted inside the beautiful home. Three stories tall. Classic Mediterranean craftsmanship. And there was always a view of the Duomo from the western windows. I wasn't sure if I would have my own bedroom, but I quickly discovered that Bartholomew intended to share his master quarters with me.

He had a private living room and a balcony, a breathtaking view of the Duomo.

I stepped onto the balcony and admired the sight. The sound of traffic came from the street below. Pigeons were on the nearby roof. In the surrounding distance was the Tuscan countryside, the Mediterranean homes perched on hills with vineyards and olive groves right on their property.

I used to walk these streets every day. Used to pick up my favorite bread in the morning, stop for an espresso in the square, ride my bike to school. My whole life had been here, and I would always feel a pain in my heart when I remembered it. My mother had loved living in Florence. Instead of having the servants grab our produce from the market, she would do it herself, picking out all the best ingredients she wanted, carrying it all home. We would get lunch afterward, working up an appetite just from thinking about all the food we would make.

I must have stood there for a while, because Bartholomew appeared at my side in just his sweatpants, his hair slightly damp like he'd hopped in the shower and washed off the plane ride.

"I love your home."

His hands rested on the rail in front of him.

"How long have you had it?"

"Five years."

"You come here often?"

"No." He stared at the Duomo, a sight that never got old.

"My old apartment isn't too far away."

"And your father?"

"He isn't too far away either." We had a summer home in the heart of Tuscany, somewhere to retreat when all the tourists came. But he preferred spending his time in the city, in the center of all the hustle. It was the most convenient way to do business.

"Would you like to take a walk?"

I looked at him, surprised by the invitation.

"We can get a coffee."

"I thought you had work to do."

"Tomorrow." He headed back inside to get dressed. "Not tonight."

When we returned to his bedroom, dinner was set on the terrace. It was sunset, the sky a beautiful combination of pastel colors. It was a little cooler out now, so I pulled on a jacket before I sat at the table.

Bartholomew poured the wine then started to eat, his eyes on the city in front of us.

Every interaction we'd had before this had been about fucking—nothing else. We'd spent the entire day together, walking the streets I used to know with our coffees in hand, and now we had a private dinner on his terrace. It was probably the most romantic date I'd ever been on—especially since I knew I'd come at the end of it.

We sat at the small table and ate, our chairs slightly turned toward the Duomo, spending our evening in silence. The chef had prepared two Florentine steaks for us, a Tuscan delicacy that I hadn't had in a very long time.

"Have you been inside the church?" I asked.

"Yes. Have you?"

"I've been on a tour inside. It's beautiful. Imagine having a wedding there…"

"You don't seem like a church wedding kind of woman."

"Well, that's where I had my first wedding."

Bartholomew turned to look at me.

I drank from my glass, remembering my wedding day like it was yesterday. I was young at the time, stupidly believing my father knew best. I was gullible and naïve, not the woman I was today.

"Will he be there?"

"My ex?"

He continued to stare.

"I'm sure he will."

Bartholomew's stare was rigid, the coldness deep in his eyes. "Will you speak?"

"It'd be awkward if we didn't."

"Then you're still on good terms."

"I wouldn't say that...given that we haven't spoken since the day I left. He's probably remarried by now."

Bartholomew looked away, staring out across the terrace again. "You must be nervous."

"I don't get nervous. At least, not about stuff like that."

"Then what does make you nervous?"

I stared at the side of his face, feeling the quickening of my heart just from admiring his handsomeness. "Can't think of anything off the top of my head."

The second we left the terrace and entered the bedroom, he was on me. He gripped me from behind, tugged me hard into his chest, and then sealed his lips over my neck like he had fangs to sink into my flesh. His tongue tasted me, his fingers dug into my soft stomach, and he ground his hard-on against the small of my back.

Like he'd wanted me all his life but had never had the chance to make me his, he yanked my shirt over my head then tugged off my bra, nearly ripping the elastic because he was so harsh. The rest of my clothes fell. His did too.

And then I was on my back on the bed, the terrace doors still wide open, the city lights stretching across us. He got on top of me, folded me beneath him, and then crushed his mouth to mine as he took me in a single thrust.

I gave a gasp as I dug my nails into his back.

His face rested against my cheek as he fucked me, his warm breaths falling against my skin. His moans were loud in my ear. His dick somehow felt bigger and harder. He took me like a prize after a conquered land. Fucked me like a whore but made me feel like a queen.

In record time, I reached my first climax, the pleasure so long and potent that I felt several shivers up my spine. It was so good, and I didn't feel the least bit rushed because this man had proven he could handle watching me come without blowing his load.

He positioned himself over me, his strong arms hooking my knees back so he could pound into my pussy and rock the headboard. His eyes were locked on mine, seeing the residual heat from the climax he'd just given me. "Fuck, sweetheart..."

It was the first time I slept beside him.

Sometimes I would wake up in the middle of the night when I rolled over, and he would be there. And sometimes he wouldn't. When the morning sunlight came through the terrace doors, he was beside me.

Dead asleep, the sheets at his waist, turned over on his stomach, with his hands underneath the pillow. His back was exposed, tight and muscular. His chest rose and fell slowly as he slept on.

I leaned in and pressed a kiss to his shoulder before I got out of bed and showered. He had a hallway that led to his master bathroom, far away from where he slept so I wouldn't wake him up. I spent the next hour and a half doing my hair and makeup, getting ready to see people I hadn't seen in nearly ten years.

In nothing but one of the robes that hung in the bathroom, I returned to the bedroom to find Bartholomew was awake. He sat on the terrace in nothing but his sweatpants, drinking coffee and reading the newspaper.

I stepped outside. "I didn't wake you, did I?"

He lowered the paper and looked at me, his eyes focused on the tie of my robe. "I told you I had business."

"But I thought you conducted your business at night."

He continued to stare at my stomach as if he didn't hear a word I said. Then he tugged one side of the tie, making the material loosen around my waist and my robe partially open. The skin of my stomach was revealed, the inside swell of my tits too. His hand moved up my thigh to my ass, and he leaned in and pressed a kiss to my bare skin. "Have some breakfast." He pushed the chair beside him from underneath the table, making it slide out so I could sit.

With a spread of cheeses and fresh croissants and fruit, I couldn't say no. I took a seat, basking in the morning light, and watched him pour me a cup of coffee. He leaned back in the chair and went back to reading his newspaper.

We sat quietly, enjoying our breakfast in the comfortable silence between two people well acquainted with each other. The coffee was exquisite, along with the aged cheeses and fresh honey, but my stomach was in waves at the moment. "I wish you could come with me."

He lowered the newspaper and looked at me.

I didn't even realize what I'd said until I said it.

"I can—if that's what you want."

"No...my father would interrogate me about you."

"You don't have to answer his questions as it's none of his business."

"It's just not the time or place. I'm there to pay my respects...not draw attention to myself."

Bartholomew stared with his hard gaze, keeping his thoughts to himself. "And what will you say if your ex asks if you're seeing anybody?"

"I doubt he'll ask."

"And if he does?" he pressed.

"The truth," I finally said with a shrug. "That I'm getting the best sex of my life..." I said it with my gaze averted, not because of the shame, but because it was meaningless.

He didn't gloat or smile, like he was used to hearing that kind of praise. After the volume of sex he must have had in his life, it was no surprise that he could fuck so well.

I took a couple bites of food, washed it down with my coffee, and then stepped back inside to get dressed.

His voice came from behind me. "Would you like some of the best sex of your life before you go?" He stood there in his gray sweatpants, low on his hips, his abs so chiseled against that hard body. Now he grinned, with an almost boyish charm.

I dropped the robe from my shoulders as I faced him, standing there in nothing but my thong. "Please."

12

BARTHOLOMEW

I was tired.

These were not my normal working hours, waking up in the morning, the sun high in the sky and beating down on my face. I took the car from the garage and made my escape from Florence into the countryside of Tuscany. Springtime greenery was everywhere, motorbikes enjoying the open road before the tourist season. Cypress trees marked the driveways to Italian villas from the main road. It was a forty-five-minute drive into wine country, to the countryside of Siena.

I pulled off the main road and entered a dirt path. Dust flew past me in my wake. Olive trees became more abundant as I approached the one-story farmhouse and the acreage of land that produced some of the best Italian wine I'd ever had.

I parked my car and let myself inside.

Wine tasting was being held on the outside terrace by a woman who held on to her beauty despite her middle age. I moved down the hallway to the office that I wanted, and when I stepped inside, I saw a man I didn't recognize.

He'd been on his phone, but now he looked at me with steel-blue eyes, cloudy with suspicion and threat. He seemed to know who I was—or what I was—without asking me a single question. He slowly rose to his feet, presenting himself as a powerful man, ink marked all over his arms, a black wedding ring on his left hand. He was built like a brick shithouse, like he ate an ox every morning for breakfast then picked up a truck.

"I'm looking for Crow."

He came around the desk and slowly approached me. "And who are you?"

"Bartholomew."

"I asked who you are—not your name."

This guy used to be in the game too. Must have retired once he got married. "We have a mutual friend."

"Crow has been out of the game for decades."

"And I'm not asking him to come back. Just need a favor."

The guy sized me up before he walked past me, purposely hitting me in the shoulder as he passed. On his way out, he bent down and stuck his hand underneath a table, pulling out a pistol stowed out of sight. "Wait here."

There were several buildings to the winery because they grew their harvest and processed it on-site. We walked across the gravel between buildings, far away from the wine tasting being conducted outside the restaurant, and entered a storage facility with barrels stacked on shelves fifty feet in the air.

Crow appeared from behind one of the shelves, in a black t-shirt and dark jeans. His olive skin reminded me of Laura's, and his dark eyes reminded me of bullets. For a man who could be my father, he looked just as in shape as I was. His eyes were just as ruthless too, seeing right through me. "I left that life before my children were born. It's been over thirty years, but somehow, random men like you still show up from time to time." He came close, his intelligent eyes challenging mine. "My wife is working at the restaurant, my son-in-law is doing the books, and my brother is in the bottling room—and you think it's wise to provoke me?"

I liked this guy. He still had the swagger of a gangster. "I wanted to ask a favor."

"I don't owe you anything, asshole."

I gave a slight smile. "For being out of the game, you seem to know exactly who I am."

"I live a quiet life—but I don't bury my head in the sand. Now leave my property, or I'll put a bullet in your stomach."

I ignored what he said. "You're going to Antonio's funeral today?"

Crow stared at me for a solid three seconds. "Yes."

I could tell his son-in-law revered him, just from the way he looked at him, the way he stood beside him like they were allies on a battlefield.

"Why?" Crow asked.

"I need you to get me some information."

Crow's eyes narrowed. "I said I don't owe you anything. And don't try to buy me off—because that won't work either."

"I have nothing to offer a man who has everything."

"Then we're finished," Crow said. "Leave."

"But I'm trying to help someone, and I think that might matter to you."

Crow stared at me, standing at my height, his sleeves tight on his muscular arms. "If it's not a member of my family, I couldn't care less."

"Someone very close to me was raped by a couple of guys. I'm trying to track them down, but since it's been seven years, I need some leads."

Crow had no reaction.

"It's Leonardo's daughter, Laura. And I have a feeling Leonardo didn't do a damn thing about it."

Crow still didn't react.

"I know what happened to your sister. I know this is a cause that's important to you. All I need are the names—and I'll do the rest."

He had the best poker face I'd ever seen. "I don't think this is appropriate to mention at a funeral."

"It's my only option."

After a long stare, Crow finally gave a nod. "I'll get what you need."

"Thank you."

The man always looked angry, even when his face seemed to be at rest. His eyes bored into mine like he was just as pissed off as at the start of this conversation. "I'm not doing it for you."

13

LAURA

I walked through the streets as I made my way to the church. Without looking at a map, I knew exactly how to get there, because it was just a mile from Bartholomew's home and I knew this area of the city like I knew my own body.

When I rounded the corner, I saw the hearse at the curb, saw all the people in black filing inside while the sounds of organ music mixed with the traffic. Greeting everyone was my aunt Rebecca, in a black dress and shawl, her son Alex beside her.

My father was also there in his black suit, looking fit other than the small belly he carried. His beard had lots of gray in it now. He had wrinkles in the corners of his eyes that hadn't been there before. He seemed shorter too. But his presence was everything I remembered. The way he exuded power effortlessly—and also instilled fear.

I wore a black pencil skirt and a white blouse with pumps. Wearing heels all day, every day had made me a pro at sporting them down the streets of Florence. When I reached the sidewalk, I felt my heart tumble into my stomach. As much as I tried to remain fearless, the anxiety was potent. It was like taking a shot of absinthe. It burned as it slid down my throat—and then frothed in my stomach.

I approached them.

My father was the first one to notice me. He turned to regard me, his dark eyes taking me in with an indifferent expression. It seemed to take him a moment to recognize me. I liked my dark hair and I never dyed it, so that wasn't different. He must have noticed that I had aged as much as he did. Now I was a woman—and not a girl he could push around.

Aunt Rebecca looked at me, taking in my appearance with the same reservations.

My father looked into my eyes for a while, his stare shifting back and forth. "My daughter—beautiful as ever." His hand went to my arm, and he leaned in to kiss me on the cheek.

I didn't move an inch.

He stepped back, not offended by my coldness, as if he'd been expecting it.

I looked at Aunt Rebecca. "I'm so sorry about Uncle Tony. He was a good man."

Her eyes instantly watered, like his death was still a fresh wound.

Alex gripped her by the shoulder and escorted her inside.

My father slid his hands into his pockets as he regarded me. "I'm glad you came." Traffic passed us on the street, but it was silenced by our conversation. No one else approached the church, like everyone who wanted to come was already packed inside.

I gave a nod—and walked inside.

The church was enormous, but every seat was filled. A lot of the men were those who worked for my father, and the rest were family and friends. Like true Italians, our families ran big, and our love even bigger.

Too bad most of them were fucking criminals.

Most of my family was Catholic, so it was a long service. Lots of prayers.

Aunt Rebecca cried through most of it. So did her son and daughter, cousins that I wasn't close to.

When the service ended, people had the option to attend the celebration of life held at my father's estate or join the family to lay my uncle to rest at the cemetery outside the city. Everyone filed out as they made their decisions.

People turned to look at me, giving me double takes, like they weren't sure if I was who they thought I was.

I felt like an outsider in my own family, either because I got divorced, which was forbidden, because I was raped, or because I'd been estranged from my father for so long. Whatever the reason, it made me wish Bartholomew were beside me, his arm over the back of my chair, making me feel wanted when no one else did.

"Laura."

I recognized his voice without seeing his face. I was still seated in the aisle, cornered, so I couldn't pretend he wasn't there and walk away. I decided to take the high road and rise to my feet to look him dead in the eye. "Victor."

He took in my features, his eyes shifting back and forth between mine, looking at me the way my father did, like he knew I looked different but couldn't pinpoint why. He was still tall and handsome, and seven years of age had given him a more rugged look. Even in his suit jacket, the muscles were undeniable. "Been a long time."

Not long enough. "How are you?" I asked, doing my best to pretend I actually cared.

He seemed to see right through it because he didn't answer. "I'm sorry about your uncle. Your father took it pretty hard."

"Really? He seems fine to me."

He gave a slight shrug. "Not the kind of man to wear his heart on his sleeve."

"You'd think he'd make an exception for his brother."

When Victor felt my hostility, he started to back away. "You don't have to stay in Paris because of me."

"*Because of you?*" I asked, unable to control my laugh. "Don't flatter yourself, Victor. I wanted a new life, a life away from my father, and I can proudly say I have one. I own my own business, and my hot-as-fuck boyfriend doesn't care that I was gang-raped by some assholes."

He gave a slight flinch, either uncomfortable by my crassness or ashamed by my words. "When your father said you were coming, I was actually hoping I'd get a chance to talk to you about that."

"What's there to say, Victor?"

His eyes locked on mine, like he rose above his embarrassment to be sincere. "I'm sorry about the way I behaved. I didn't handle it very well—"

"You *dumped* me, Victor. While I was going through the hardest thing in my life, you were wondering if you'd ever want to fuck me again."

He cringed, his eyes closing like he couldn't look at me as he heard that.

"And when you couldn't, you divorced me. That was how you handled it."

He stared down at the floor for a while, like my gaze was too hard to meet. "It was more complicated than that, but you're right, I didn't handle it well...and I'm very sorry. I married too young, before I really knew what it takes to be a husband. I've grown a lot since we last spoke...and I've carried this regret ever since."

"So you want me to forgive you?" I asked coldly. "So you can clear your conscience?"

He lifted his eyes again. "I don't deserve your forgiveness. But I want you to have my apology."

"You know, this would have meant a lot more. I don't know...six or seven years ago."

He gave a slight nod. "I knew you didn't want to talk to me."

"And you think that's changed?"

His eyes turned rigid, and he swallowed.

"It hasn't."

The cemetery was full of olive trees, an open landscape with the hills in full view. It was a beautiful place to sleep for eternity. It was a warm afternoon, but the breeze was kind enough to lick the sweat from our skin.

The priest continued the service at the gravesite as we all stood around. Aunt Rebecca sobbed into her black handkerchief while her son stood at her side, devoid of all emotion like that would make it easier for his mother. My father stood with his hands in his pockets, looking at the midnight-black coffin with a pearl shine, lifeless as a stone, as if losing his only brother was just another day on the job.

I knew I looked emotionless as well, but that was due to the company.

The casket was lowered. Everyone grabbed a handful of white lilies and tossed them on top. Uncle Tony was buried with the love of his friends and family. It was a beautiful and painful sight, but all I could think about was how he'd been killed.

There was no rosary. No open casket. Suspicious for Catholics.

He was probably butchered beyond repair—and everyone knew it.

Aunt Rebecca continued to sob at the gravesite, sitting in one of the white chairs as the sun hit her back. Alex was now the man of the family, and he seemed to take that role seriously by never leaving her side.

As the crowd started to thin, my eyes found a face similar to mine.

Dark hair. Green eyes. Both timid and skittish. She held my gaze like she was as mesmerized by me as I was by her. Seven years since I'd last seen her face or even a photo of her. When I left, she was a girl. But now...she was a woman.

A married woman. A diamond ring was on her left hand, and a man in a suit stood beside her. He was a good-looking guy, but his eyes were unkind. He looked like someone who could easily be cruel.

He turned away, tugging her arm slightly as he guided her from the gravesite.

That was when the sun hit her face like a spotlight.

And I saw it—the black eye.

It had to be several days old because it was faint, faint enough that makeup could hide it well in normal light. But the second she turned fully into the sun, it was like a slide under a microscope, a criminal under the spotlight.

My father's estate was grand, shiny with shameless greed. Three stories with a large courtyard, something unheard of in the heart of Florence, and an entire maid service at his beck and call—for a single man.

Uncle Tony's blood paid for this place.

Most people were gathered in the courtyard where large olive trees stood tall in their pots. Streams of lights crossed the area, ready to illuminate the party once the sun was gone. Waiters came around and served wine and cocktails to guests who stood and chatted. Others sat at the round tables with white tablecloths and ate their dinner. A fountain with flowing water stood in the center of it all, the sound accompanied by quiet music over the speakers.

How are you, sweetheart?

Despite how shitty the day was, that message managed to tug my lips into a smile. *Been better, vampire.*

I've been called a few names in my lifetime. Never that one.

It suits you.

I'm awake now, aren't I?

Got me there. I grabbed a glass of wine from a waiter and moved to one of the open tables. Dinner was being served, but I wasn't hungry.

There was a pause, like he expected me to say something. And when I didn't, he typed another message. *What happened?*

For a man so heartless, he was awfully attentive. *Too much for text. But I'm about to punch some asshole in the face.*

You want me to do it for you?

I knew he was serious. *No. I have a nice round hook.*

You have a nice round ass too.

I released a quiet laugh then covered it quickly, knowing it wasn't the time or place for that.

What'd he do?

My little sister has a black eye. And I think I know who gave it to her.

It's always the boyfriend.

Husband, actually.

I didn't know you had a sister.

It's complicated…

Call me if you need me, sweetheart. I'll give him more than just a black eye.

He was the sunlight on a cloudy day. A piece of joy in sorrow. He was just a man I was fucking, but now, he'd become a lot more.

A friend…

So I wouldn't stick out like a sore thumb, I grabbed a plate of dinner and sat alone at the table. People talked in quiet voices, remembering Uncle Tony and his loud voice at all the parties. They all pretended that this funeral was timely, that he wasn't killed for pushing drugs and my father's agenda.

Disgusting.

The waiter took my dirty plate, and I crossed the courtyard to grab another glass of wine.

"Laura." My father's voice commanded my attention. It brought back childhood memories, when he would call my name just so he could tell me to do something. Not do my chores, but fetch him another scotch.

I turned back around and made a slow approach, feeling so much hatred in my racing heart. My eyes were locked on his, ignoring the men who stood with him.

"This is my daughter Laura." My father introduced me to two men who were clearly brothers. Same dark hair. Same olive complexion. Same dark eyes. They both regarded me with interest, like they already knew my story. "Laura, this is Crow and Cane Barsetti. Old family friends."

Crow stared me down like the scope of a sniper. Didn't blink. Didn't speak or try to shake my hand. The look was so intense, it was like he hated me. The brother behaved the same way, looking at me like horns had grown out of my skull.

I spoke to break the tension. "I haven't spoken to Vanessa in a while. How is she?" We used to be friends, but after I moved away, it became harder to keep in touch. She had her family and her priorities, so she didn't travel much. And of course, I'd never returned to Italy until now.

The second I mentioned his daughter, the tightness in Crow's face released. Now his eyes shifted back and forth between mine, regarding me with a whole new attitude. "She's well. Back at work now that my grandchildren are in school."

"Good for her," I said. "She's such a talented artist."

He gave a nod. "Yes, she is." There was a hint of pride in his voice. A moment ago, he looked like another one of my father's cronies, angry and hostile. And now, he looked like a person…a father.

My father never looked at me like that. It didn't come as a surprise, but it still hurt.

I said goodbye and dismissed myself, letting the men resume their conversation, no doubt about business. Uncle Tony was probably briefly mentioned then forgotten, already old news even though we stood at his funeral that very moment.

I spotted her across the terrace, sitting alone at the table. A waiter had just come by to pick up her dirty plate. Her little fingers wrapped around her glass of red wine, and she took a small drink. She seemed to be in a haze, not looking at anything in particular, her mind taking her somewhere else. So distracted, she didn't notice my approach until I was directly on top of her.

When her eyes found mine, they went still. She held the glass of wine to her lips with a steady hand.

I took a seat, keeping a chair between us.

She slowly lowered the glass back to the table.

The tension between us was so heavy, it was like we held each other at gunpoint. Her feelings toward me were as clear as a billboard in Times Square. She'd heard all the rumors about me, had formed an opinion based on whatever bullshit my father said whenever someone asked about me. There was such an age gap between us that she was too young to really know me. Now she was twenty-one but still looked like a teenager, too young to be married, just the way I'd been before my father pushed Victor on me.

I suspected he'd done the same to her—even though he was the world's worst matchmaker. "How are you, Catherine?"

After a long stare, she gave a shrug. "Fine, I guess."

"I didn't know you got married." I knew my invitation didn't get lost in the mail. It was never sent. She never called me. Didn't even text. I stopped trying years ago because she ignored every olive branch I extended.

What kind of father turned his daughters against each other?

She never addressed what I said.

"Father arranged it?"

She finally gave a nod.

My eyes focused on her face, hardly noticing the color of her left eye. "No amount of makeup is going to hide that."

Her reaction was instant, terror crossing her beautiful features.

"Does Father know?"

Her eyes dropped, and now I wouldn't get a peep out of her.

"Leave him, Catherine."

Her eyes stayed down.

"Come with me to Paris. You don't have to stay here."

She looked up again. "Marriage is forever, Laura."

"Not when your husband is an asshole, honey. You don't owe him shit."

She looked away, probably looking at Father across the courtyard. "It's complicated—"

"It's not complicated. I remember how I was when I was your age. I remember feeling the pressure to do whatever Father wanted. But I can tell you it doesn't need to be that way. He doesn't own you."

"Lucas is one of Father's most trusted men. He hand-picked him for me—"

"It's just a power move, Catherine. To keep you under his thumb."

"He bought us a beautiful apartment as a wedding gift—"

"To control you. Nothing he does is out of love. It's manipulation."

Her eyes glanced past me, right over my shoulder, like she made eye contact with someone. "I shouldn't talk to you…"

"Your own sister?" I asked incredulously.

Her eyes came back to me. "You humiliated Father—"

"I humiliated *him*?" My voice rose over the music, and I didn't try to contain it. "Oh, that's rich."

Her eyes were past my shoulder again. "I-I have to go." She rose from the chair and left the table, leaving me to sit there alone.

I grabbed her abandoned wineglass and drank the rest of it before I looked behind me.

Catherine was at my father's side, his arm around her shoulders, like he'd just beckoned her to come over and she'd obeyed—like a fucking dog. He continued his conversation with the Barsetti brothers.

I excused myself from the shitshow and entered the house. It was the same house I'd grown up in, so I knew my way around, knew the parlor was down the hallway past the kitchen. The cigar smoke announced the men in the room before I stepped inside. Four guys sat in the armchairs, making themselves at home with my father's cigars and scotch. One of them was Victor, and the smile that was on his face just moments ago was wiped off as if I'd slapped him. I didn't pay him much attention, though, because my eyes were reserved for my brother-in-law.

He stilled when my gaze settled on him, quickly realizing the bullets in my eyes were meant for him.

"I don't think we've met," I said as I sauntered across the room toward him. "I'm Laura." I plucked the cigar out of his fingers and stabbed it down onto his exposed forearm.

He screamed before he swung his arm, getting the hot ash off his skin. There was already a distinct burn in his dark skin, a scar he would now carry for the rest of his life. "You cunt." He was on his feet, facing off with me like he would swing at my face.

"Oh, I wouldn't do that if I were you." Bartholomew's face came into my mind, granting me his protection even though he wasn't even in the room. "Because my boyfriend will skin you alive then hang your body outside the Duomo."

That made him falter, but only momentarily. He grabbed me by the shoulder and raised his fist to pummel me in the face.

"Oh good, now I'll have a black eye to match my sister's."

Victor put himself between us, his hand on the arm of his friend. "Let it go."

The guy huffed and puffed, like an angry bull in the streets of Pamplona.

"I'm not gonna let it go," I snapped. "Hurt my sister again, and you'll regret it, I promise you."

He spat at my feet. "Why don't you take a walk down a dark alleyway and get raped again—"

Victor punched him so hard in the face that he was knocked out cold. His body fell on the rug in front of the two armchairs. Then Victor looked at me, breathing hard, studying my face to make sure I was okay.

I kept a straight face as I walked over to his unconscious body, feeling Victor's angry stare on my face. I lifted my heel and stepped down right on his crotch. He was so out of it he didn't feel it, but when he woke up, he would definitely feel the bite of my heel then.

Victor walked beside me as I exited the property.

"I don't need an escort, Victor." I didn't say goodbye to my father, to anyone else I'd made small talk with. It was the strangest feeling—to feel welcomed and cast out at the same time.

I was on the sidewalk outside the estate, and for the first time, my heels started to bother me. It'd been a long day

—a very long day. Instead of taking a cab, I decided to walk, because I needed the time to process all that bullshit before I walked into the room with Bartholomew.

I wasn't sure what I would share and what I would omit.

"That was a really fucked-up thing to say—"

"I don't care what he said, Victor." Now I knew how everyone saw me. Damaged. Irreparable. Dirty. Did they expect me to take on four men by myself? A little hard without a gun.

"Well, I do. I'll handle it."

"Like the way you handled our divorce?" I asked, rounding on him.

He gave a little cringe.

The guilt swept through me, because in that moment, I realized Victor was the only one on my side. He was the only one being remotely nice to me. Everyone else, my own family, basically told me to fuck off. "I shouldn't have said that…"

His eyes remained averted for a while.

"Why would my father choose him for his daughter?"

His mind seemed to be elsewhere because he took a while to respond. "He's loyal."

"Aren't all of you loyal?"

"But he's the favorite. A couple years ago, some stuff went down... Lucas was the one who stayed. Took a bullet for your father."

Wow, they were perfect for each other. "Does my father know Lucas hurts his daughter?" I asked the question even though I already had the answer.

"You know how traditional he is..."

Now I wondered if he'd hurt my mother too. "I gotta get my sister out of there."

"You can't help someone who doesn't want to be helped."

"She's too young to know better." And Lucas seemed to be close to thirty, based on my guess.

He gave a shrug. "Maybe when she gets older she'll feel differently."

"But by then, it'll be too late." She'd have a kid. Maybe two. Then she'd be trapped for good.

Victor stared at me, an old look he used to give me. "Can I take you home—"

"I can get there on my own." For the most part, Bartholomew didn't seem like the jealous type, especially when I wasn't his in the first place, but it would still be awkward if he saw my ex-husband drop me off.

I wanted to ask Victor to keep an eye on my sister, but he'd done such a terrible job taking care of me that I knew he wasn't capable of the task. And it wasn't his problem either.

"I'm really glad I saw you today." He said it without looking at me, like he didn't want to see the hatred in my eyes. "That you're doing well."

"Yeah, you too."

When I returned to the house, Bartholomew was talking on the phone as he sat on the balcony, dressed in the same sweatpants as when I left. His hair was styled now, and his arms had a red flush to them, so it seemed as if he'd worked out and showered while I was gone. When he realized I was there, he stopped everything he was doing. "I'll call you back, Bleu." He set the phone down and rose to his full height, six-foot-something of all man, looking at me in the special way of his…the way that made me feel like a woman.

He approached me in the bedroom, his eyes searching my face for distress. "How are you, sweetheart?" For a man who heartlessly pushed drugs across the country, he seemed to care about every thought that crossed my mind. He was already screwing me, so it wasn't like he was trying to get me into bed with false affection. He and my father were in the same business, but they couldn't be more different.

"I think I need a drink…"

His lips lifted slightly in a smile, but his eyes remained cold. He walked to his bar, poured two scotches, on the rocks the way he liked, and we sat together in the living room, away from the heat outside.

I slipped off my heels and pulled my knees to my chest as I sat in the corner of the couch. Just the way I'd imagined at the funeral, he sat beside me, his arm over the back of the couch behind me, his knees wide apart and taking up more room than he really needed. His fingers found the hair at the nape of my neck and lightly caressed the strands as I told him about what had happened with Catherine's husband. Intense eyes examined my face, like his fingers wanted to move to the front of my throat and squeeze. "Did you punch him?"

"No. I burned his cigar into his forearm."

A subtle smile moved on to his lips, and this time, it was real. I could tell when it was forced and when it was involuntary. "That'll get the message across."

"I hope he thinks of me every time he sees it."

"I'm sure he will."

"Unfortunately, I don't think it'll change anything with my sister."

His fingers started to move through my hair again. "I can change it for you."

"As tempting as that is…it's okay."

"What did he do to you after you burned him?"

"You know, called me a bitch, stuff like that…" I wasn't sure why I omitted the truth. I guess because those words hurt more than I wanted to admit. It was easy to wear a poker face around Victor and those other assholes…but not Bartholomew.

Bartholomew studied my face, like he knew something was missing but didn't ask for more information.

"He tried to punch me, but Victor stopped him."

"Victor?"

"My ex."

His expression remained steady, but there was a subtle flash across his eyes. "So you did speak."

"A bit."

He gave a slight nod then looked away. "And how was that?"

"He tried to apologize, but I wasn't interested in listening to it. Told him I was over it, that I have a hot-as-fuck boyfriend who doesn't have a problem fucking my brains out."

His fingers stiffened in my hair, and he slowly turned his head to look at me.

"Don't worry about the boyfriend comment. I was just trying to get my point across."

He remained still, his eyes on me.

"My father seemed happy to see me...but also cold at the same time. Everyone else looked at me like I was a goddamn ghost or something. Catherine is pinned under my father's thumb, obeys him and her husband like a dog. I don't know what to do…"

"I don't think there's anything you can do."

"She's my sister… I can't just abandon her."

"She's not your responsibility."

"Well, if my mother were here, she wouldn't let this shit fly. And I won't either." At least, I think she didn't let it fly. The older I got, the more I saw my father for what he really was. Why would she have married him in the first place? Was he different when they first met? Did the money and power corrupt him later? I grabbed the scotch and took a big drink, let the burn clear my throat of all the bullshit I'd swallowed at the funeral.

"What's this guy's name?"

"Lucas. Why?"

"He tried to hit you. You thought there would be no repercussions for that?" He looked at me with that intense gaze, his jawline hard like he was ready to break a fist with his mouth.

"Victor stopped it. I told you that."

"Doesn't change anything. You don't threaten my woman and walk free."

"I provoked him—"

"Doesn't. Change. Anything."

"Bartholomew, just let it go—"

"I don't let anything go." His hand moved underneath my hair and gripped the back of my neck. The ferocity was in his dark eyes, like I was the one who was stupid enough to cross him. "Ever."

His thumbs hooked into my thong, and he pulled it down my long legs. Now I was naked on the bed, and he took his time moving up my body, kissing the insides of my knees, my thighs, and then pressing hot kisses to the area where I craved him most. His tongue expertly kissed me, tasted me, made me shed tears long before I was ready to come.

He continued upward, kissing my tummy, the skin over my ribs, and then sucking my nipples so hard it made me wince. He dragged his tongue up the valley between my breasts then kissed my collarbone. By the time his face was above mine, I was so desperate, I was about to lose my goddamn mind.

His thighs separated mine, and then his big dick sank inside me. Slow and steady, it inched into my tightness before it hit the flood of my arousal. Then it was a smooth entry, his enormous size burrowed into my smallness.

My hands scooped underneath his shoulders, and I hooked my ankles around his waist as I let him dominate me. The heat of his body sealed me in place, his weight pinning me against the mattress right where I wanted to be. My nails dug deeper because it was so good, exactly what I wanted after such a shitty day.

He rocked into me, burying himself more fully with every thrust, staring at me with a look so deep it looked like hatred.

If I hadn't had him to come home to, I wasn't sure how I would have survived this day. My fingers dug deep into his dark hair, feeling my body shift as he rocked into me, lost in a heat so searing it was like fucking on the sun.

14

BARTHOLOMEW

I reached for my phone on the nightstand.

We're ready for you.

I set the phone down and looked at the woman wrapped around me like a blanket. She used my chest as a pillow, used my body as her favorite stuffed animal to snuggle with. With tangled hair and ruined makeup, she was sexed up real good. Made it hard to leave.

I gently slipped from her grasp and replaced my body with a different pillow.

She didn't stir at all.

I grabbed my phone and walked out.

A change of clothes was in the other room, so I laced up my boots and grabbed my jacket before I got into the car waiting for me downstairs. It took me across town to one of my other properties.

It was dead of night, almost three in the morning, perfect time to be alive.

I walked inside and hit the second floor.

There they were. All four of them. Hands zip-tied behind their backs. Their ankles restrained too.

I noticed the wrench and pile of teeth on the floor. I looked at Bleu.

He gave a guilty shrug. "Warmed them up for you."

I examined the men on their knees. They seemed to know who I was because one of them pissed himself right there on the hardwood floor. "Who wants to go first?"

"I have a family." The first one in the row spoke out of terror. "A wife...three kids. Come on, please—"

"She had a husband. Did that stop you?"

He shook, and his mouth opened to speak, but nothing came out.

"You'll go first."

"Please just listen to me...two boys and a girl. What will they do if I don't come home?"

I nodded to Bleu.

My guys pushed the man over onto his side, head to the floor.

"Please!" He turned hysterical. "I'm sorry. I was just following orders—"

"A dick doesn't get hard on demand." I pressed my boot on top of his head. "It got hard because you enjoyed it. Now I'm going to enjoy this."

"No!"

Stomp. Stomp. Stomp.

His screams grew louder every time I slammed my foot down. When a crack formed in his skull, he got even louder.

Stomp. Stomp. Stomp.

He went quiet.

Stomp. Stomp. Stomp.

I kept going until the floor was a pile of bones, brains, and blood. Where a head used to be was just a scene from a nightmare. Didn't faze me at all. "Alright. Who wants to go next?"

We pulled up to the bar.

There were only a couple guys inside, drinking at four in the morning because their boss owned the place. I could see them through the dark window, sitting right at the bar with their tall glasses full of whatever piss they were drinking.

"You sure about this?" Bleu was in the back seat with me.

"Yep."

"They'll all be armed."

"And so am I."

"It's three on one—"

"I got this." I stepped out of the car and went up to the door. Of course, it was locked, but it only took a couple shoulder jabs to get the door to fly open.

The three of them were still, looking at me like I was some drunk idiot who'd wandered into the wrong bar. I straightened my jacket then approached them, and once they got a better look at me, they realized I was the real deal.

"Lucas?" I stopped in front of my opponent, the one so arrogant that he sized me up without getting off his stool.

"Who's asking?" His hand remained on his glass.

"Laura's *boyfriend*."

His eyes gave a flash.

"Looks like you've heard of me."

His hand dove inside his jacket for his gun.

I grabbed him off the chair and stabbed my knife right into his side.

He gasped as he stilled, like he could feel exactly where the blade was.

The other two men had their guns drawn, but with their comrade right in front of me, they were powerless to do anything.

I looked at both of them, knowing one of them had been married to Laura. It must be the one on the right, because he was built and good-looking—but still undeserving of her. But whether that assumption was right or not, it didn't matter right now. "All I have to do is twist this knife slightly to the left and I'll puncture your right lung. You might make it to the hospital, might not. Depends on how fast you can haul ass."

Lucas barely breathed, like he was afraid too big a breath would push up against the blade.

"You tried to hit my girl?"

Lucas was paralyzed, blood dripping down his side and soaking into his jacket and shirt.

I pushed my knife a little deeper. "You didn't think that question was rhetorical, did you?"

He ground his teeth as he groaned. "She fucked with me first—"

I pushed the knife deeper.

"Fuck, I'm sorry, alright? What do you want from me?"

"I want you to know what will happen if you try that again." I pulled the knife out in one swift movement.

Lucas practically collapsed on the floor.

I kept him upright. "Do we have an understanding?"

"Yes…Jesus Christ."

I let him fall to the floor.

The one I assumed to be Victor lowered his gun.

Smart man.

I stared at the other one, curious to see just how stupid he was.

After he glanced at Victor, he slowly lowered his weapon.

Lucas continued to groan like a slug on the floor.

I wiped my blade on his coat before I walked out.

When I walked in the door, my footsteps stirred her.

She sat up, her thick hair all over the place, her eyes squinting as she tried to see in the dark. "Bartholomew?" Her hand reached for the sheets beside her, looking for me even though she knew I wasn't there.

"Right here, sweetheart." I stripped off my clothes then got into bed beside her.

"Where—where did you go?"

"Had some things I needed to take care of." I rolled on top of her, positioning her naked body underneath me. She was still half asleep, so her body moved exactly the way I wanted it to, opening for me so I could slip between her soft thighs.

"What things...?"

I slid inside her, succumbing to her heavenly flesh instantly. My dick hardened even more, aroused that I was the only one worthy of this woman. That I was the only one who could handle a woman with this kind of fire.

The questions ceased when she felt me burrowed in her tightness. Her nails hooked into my flesh, and she writhed underneath me. The moans came immediately. The hot breaths. The sexy whispers. She grabbed my ass and tugged. "Bartholomew..."

15

LAURA

We took a shower together the next morning. We stood under the warm water, and I was lucky enough to rub soap all over his chiseled body, to trace the line of his pecs, to rub the planes of his stomach, to clean all the individual muscles of his ripped arms.

He did the same to me, making my tits and ass soapy with his big hands.

"I can't tell if you're a tit or an ass man."

His hands moved to my tits and felt them in his hands. Then he did the same to my ass, as if comparing. "With you, it's both." His fingers reached around my ass until he found my clit. He lightly played with it while his other hand gripped one of my tits. "I can't wait to fuck you in the ass."

"*Excuse me?*"

He dipped his head and kissed me, pulling me into his body as the water rained down on us. "You heard me." He stepped out of the shower and grabbed the towel before drying his hair, his tight ass and muscular back on full display. As if he hadn't just said something very presumptuous and a bit offensive, he carried on with his day, moving to the vanity to shave his beard.

I dried off then went back into the bedroom. When I checked my phone, I saw that I had ten missed calls.

All from my father.

And lots and lots of voice mails.

"Huh…that's interesting." Instead of listening to the voice mails, I called him straight back, because whatever he needed to talk about, it was important. My mind jumped to the worst-case scenario—that Lucas had killed my sister because of what I'd said to him.

He answered immediately. I wasn't even sure if it'd rung or not. "Laura."

He was pissed. I could tell just by the way he said my name. "Leonardo."

"I'm the last person you want to fuck with. I don't give a damn if you're my daughter."

"Wow, it's barely nine in the morning, and we're starting with threats already."

"Lucas is like family. How dare you do this?"

"Uh, Catherine *is* family. Why don't you care more about that?"

"What does she have to do with this?"

"*What*?" I asked incredulously. "You think some asshole can give my little sister a black eye and I'm not going to do anything about it? I'll shove a cigar in his eye next time he touches her."

He turned quiet.

"I'm not sorry, so if you're expecting an apology, you aren't going to get one."

"Laura, I'm talking about last night. Your *boyfriend* came to the bar and stabbed Lucas. Now he can barely take two steps without collapsing in pain. He's one of my best men, and I've just found myself in a crisis with one man down. This is serious."

I was quiet—because I had no idea what he was talking about.

"Give me his name." The threat was in his voice, unmistakable, full of fury.

"Don't you have a crisis on your hands?"

"Nobody touches Lucas and gets away with it."

"I literally just told you that your precious Lucas is hitting your daughter, and you act like you didn't hear it."

"Their marital problems are none of my concern—"

"Wow, you're an even bigger asshole than I thought," I snapped. "At least my man gives a damn. When I told him Lucas took a swing at me, he actually did something about it. What kind of man are you?"

"I want his name—"

"Trust me, you don't." I hung up, and just so I wouldn't have to deal with it, I turned off my phone.

"Everything okay?"

I turned around to see Bartholomew in his black sweatpants, his hair still slightly damp after drying it with a towel. His chiseled body was only blemished by a single scar, a bullet from an old friend. "You went to Lucas last night and stabbed him?"

He kept a straight face, not the least bit apologetic.

"And told them you were my boyfriend?"

He stepped closer to me, his eyes taking in mine. "You sound mad."

"Because I am."

"You wanted me to kill him?"

"No," I snapped. "I never asked you to get involved."

"Really? Because you sounded proud a minute ago."

My arms crossed over my chest. "I just wish my father... That's beside the point. Why are you going in there, telling them you're my boyfriend?"

"Because you told them I was."

"I just said that in the moment. I didn't mean it."

His eyes shifted back and forth between mine. "You told Victor, and then you told Lucas. You didn't mean it twice?"

"I was just...bragging."

"Then I guess I was bragging too."

"Do you realize the situation we're in now? My father is pissed, and he's not going to leave me alone until he finds out who you are."

"Then tell him." He carried on the conversation without raising his voice a decibel, without looking remotely flustered by the drama he'd gotten roped into. "Give him my name. Give him my address. I don't care."

I took a deep breath because I was about to explode. "If I do that, one of you will wind up dead."

"Well, you don't seem to like him, and apparently I'm not your boyfriend anymore, so..."

My arms loosened to my sides when I heard the way his tone changed. "Are you mad at me?"

"Am I your boyfriend or not?"

"I told you I just said that in the moment—"

"Then I'm not?"

"Yes."

"Then I'm mad."

"What?"

"I don't appreciate being led on."

"I didn't lead you on—"

"You said I was your *hot-as-fuck boyfriend who fucks your brains out*."

"Again, I just said that to brag, okay?"

"Really?" He stepped toward me, and now his anger took a more sinister turn. "You brag about your sex life to your father too?"

I tried to hold his gaze, but it was getting harder as he stared at me like that.

"If you really wanted to get out of this situation, you could have just said I was some lunatic obsessed with you. But you didn't. You called me your man—*and said it like you meant it*."

I kept my stance, but it was becoming more difficult. This man had always been on my side of the battlefield, but now he was my opponent, and it was a different side to him I didn't recognize.

"Did you?"

"Did I what—"

"*Mean it.*" His voice was quiet, but so deep it was like a cavern. His eyes cut right into me.

"Look, we both agreed this was just—"

"I know what we agreed to. I have a damn good memory. Now, answer my question. Am I your man or not?"

My eyes finally broke contact because I couldn't look at him anymore. "No."

His reaction was a mystery because I wasn't looking at him. But I could feel his anger, feel the way it spread across the room like the heater had just kicked on during a winter night. The longer the silence continued, the more I felt pressured to speak.

"I told you I didn't want to be with a criminal—"

"I know what you said." He stepped away, turning his back to me as he approached the terrace.

"I'm sorry—"

"Don't be. I'm used to it."

It was like he'd stabbed me in the stomach. I remembered his story about the only woman he ever loved…and how he wasn't good enough for her parents. She'd dumped him and married someone else. "It's nothing personal—"

"Sweetheart, I'm going to enlighten you." He turned back around and looked at me, and now his face was devoid of all emotion. "You think an accountant or a banker or a construction worker would have taken care of your business for you? You think any of them have the balls to handle a woman like you? You don't want a criminal, but that's exactly what you need, Laura. I'm exactly the kind of man you need. You aren't better than me, sweetheart."

"I never said I was better than you, okay? I just don't want to end up chopped into little pieces like my mother—"

"And you think I'd ever let that happen to you?" he asked incredulously. "You know what else I did last night?"

I didn't have a clue.

"I rounded up all those worthless assholes who touched you seven years ago, and I killed each and every one of them."

All I could do was breathe. I was in such shock.

"You think a goddamn accountant could do that?" He walked to the dresser and pulled out a shirt, like he needed to take off somewhere.

"You don't understand, Bartholomew…"

He pulled on the shirt, grabbed his phone, and prepared to leave the bedroom.

"Just listen to me, okay?" I didn't want him to leave. Just the thought of his absence made me panic.

He stilled but didn't look at me.

"I don't like my father…because he's more than just an asshole. I don't like him because—"

"I know why."

My eyes searched his face, waiting for him to meet my look.

He turned and locked his gaze to mine. "I know who he is. I know what kind of life you had growing up. I've known for a very long time. But the difference between your father and me is I actually give a damn about you." He turned to the door to walk out. "And don't pretend you haven't figured that out."

I waited for him to come home all day, but he never showed. I wasn't sure where he'd run off to, especially when he was just dressed in sweatpants and a t-shirt. He could have checked in to a hotel. Or maybe he owned another property here. The man was rich like my father, and rich men tended to use their money on homes they used once, maybe twice, a year. I got bored sitting there alone, so I went into the city to get something to eat, to enjoy an Americano at my favorite café.

I didn't call.

He didn't call. No surprise there.

When we came face-to-face, I wasn't sure what we would say to each other. I suspected our relationship, situationship, hookup, whatever you wanted to call it, was now over.

And that hurt.

At sunset, I returned to his home and made my way upstairs to his bedroom. When I walked inside, I realized he had come back. The terrace door was wide open, and the colors of the sky were beautiful pastels.

He sat in the living room in the clothes he'd worn when he left, one arm over the back of the couch, one ankle resting on the opposite knee. His gaze was turned toward the TV, a black screen that showed his dark reflection. After a moment of staring, he turned his attention on me, like he'd heard me the moment I'd come up the stairs.

His gaze was paralyzing, so I stood there and absorbed his poisonous stare. My heart raced as quickly as it did in the heat of our fight. I was normally calm and self-assured, but he turned me into someone who suffered silent panic attacks.

He gave a subtle gesture toward the other couch, a simple movement of his head.

I did as he asked and took a seat. The strap of my purse slipped off my shoulder. Uneasy, I ran my fingers through my hair, pulling it away from my face, fidgeting because his silent stare was like a thorn in my side.

After a long moment, he spoke. "We don't need to have that conversation to know we want different things in life. You want to marry Mr. Nice Guy and pop out a couple of kids, and I want to run the greatest drug empire Europe has ever seen. I'll never tell you I love you. I'll never ask you to marry me. I'll never give up what I've built for any woman—not even you." He stared at me with that hard face, looking as heartless as his words sounded. "But I think we're more than just two people fucking. I think I'm a deeper part of your life than you give me credit for. Do you agree?"

There was no future for us. I already knew this, but hearing him say it so bluntly stung like salt in an old wound. Bartholomew wasn't marriage material, and once I found a man who was, I would walk away. I would marry him and ignore thoughts of Bartholomew when they popped up at the most random times…when I was making dinner in the kitchen…when I dropped off the kids at school… And Bartholomew would be doing the same thing he'd always done—assuming he was still alive at that point. "Yes."

He stared at me hard, like he knew a tide of thoughts had just swept over me. "Then I'm your man. You're my woman. Until we part ways."

I gave a slight nod.

"Then this conversation is over." He leaned forward and grabbed the glass of scotch sitting there. He tilted his head back and downed the rest before he licked his lips. "Let's go out to dinner." He left the couch and entered his walk-in closet. A moment later, he returned, dressed in his signature black clothes, his short sleeves showing his nice arms.

It was a little harder for me to snap out of the moment. He'd said nothing I didn't already know, but it hit a little different this time. Now I couldn't stop admiring the sharpness of his jawline, couldn't stop thinking about the lips I kissed every day. I used to not care when this relationship ended. It was just sex, nothing more. But I suddenly cherished those moments more, the way he moved across the room, the way he looked at me like I was all he ever wanted. I cherished them because I knew they wouldn't last forever.

They would end—and it would hurt.

16

BARTHOLOMEW

It took some time to shake off the conversation. Lots of awkward silences. Uncomfortable stares. We both thought of the same thing at the same time, but neither one of us would draw attention to it.

After a couple glasses of wine and once our entrees arrived, the tension started to fade.

"This is one of my favorite restaurants," she said, cutting into her chicken.

"Mine too."

"My family came here to celebrate my eighth birthday."

It was hard to picture that, not when her father was such a prick.

"My sister was just a baby at the time. I remember she cried the entire time…" She gave a chuckle then took a bite of her food.

I took a few sips of my wine and ate my food sparingly, not having much of an appetite after I'd drunk so much throughout the day. I'd spent my time at my other property, the maids still working to get all the blood out of the hardwood floor.

Laura stared at me across the table, her plump lips painted a deep red like the color of her wine. Her eyelashes were naturally thick, and I loved the color of her hair, the color of midnight. "How did you kill them?" She kept her voice down so the other tables wouldn't hear, not that I had anything to hide.

"It was quick."

Her eyes searched mine, like she wanted more. "You didn't have to do that—"

"Yes, I did." I wanted to kill their wives too, break open their skulls while their husbands watched. But that was too barbaric—even for me. And that wasn't justice either. That was just psychotic revenge.

"It doesn't change what happened—"

"They deserved what they got. All I should be hearing from you is thank you."

"I am grateful, but...did they have families?" She searched my gaze for the answer.

I never lied, but I knew the truth would do more harm than good. "I didn't ask. Even if they did, it wouldn't have changed anything." And it didn't change anything.

Her eyes dropped down to her wineglass, but she didn't take a drink.

Her father was powerful like I was. He could have handled this a long time ago. The fact that he didn't, the fact that he didn't care that his son-in-law beat his daughter, that he let his wife be raped and murdered, told me exactly how he felt toward women in general. They were the lesser sex. They were unimportant. Nothing more than cattle.

"What exactly happened with Lucas?"

"I stabbed him. Close enough to his lung to know I meant business, but far enough away that he could still breathe. I would have killed him, but I knew you wouldn't have wanted that."

"I don't know…after seeing my sister's black eye, I might kill him myself."

So, she showed mercy toward the men who wronged her…but felt none toward men who hurt people she loved. Good thing she had me to care about her since no one else seemed to. "I can finish the job if you want."

"No…my sister would just hate me. She probably already does, actually."

I'd just made a mess of her life, but I still didn't regret getting involved. If Lucas thought he could give Laura a black eye like he did her sister, he was about to lose more than his lungs.

"Fuck…I don't know what to do."

"About?"

"This whole mess with my father."

"I told you I can handle it." We were going to come face-to-face eventually. I didn't want to pull the trigger too soon when I had a much bigger plan for that asshole, but I wouldn't shy away from a fight either.

"I don't want these two parts of my life to mix. They need to stay separate—exactly as they belong." She held up both of her hands in opposite directions, like she was the one in the middle of the chaos. "I'll have to talk to him." She lowered her hands and grabbed her glass of wine.

"I'm not sorry for what I did, but I'm sorry if I made your life complicated."

She took a drink as she stared at me, her little throat shifting as she swallowed. When the glass was returned to the table, she licked her lips absent-mindedly, like she had no idea how every little thing she did turned me on. "I know, Bartholomew."

When we returned to the house, the maid had tidied up the bedroom, had completed her turn-down service with the sheets pulled back, the lights dimmed, a glass of water on each nightstand.

She took a seat on the couch and slipped off her heels. "It's like living in a hotel."

I undressed, leaving my boots in the closet and returning my knife to the drawer.

"Your place in Paris must really be something."

Places. I came back into the bedroom in my boxers, seeing her in just her lacy white bra and matching underwear. Black had always been my favorite color, but she made me second-guess that. It was beautiful against her olive skin, her midnight-dark hair, the deep color of her lips.

Her gaze caught mine, and she must have understood the meaning in my look because her eyes turned guarded, like they always did when she was nervous around me. She used to be so confident, pushing me back and straddling my hips, but now her breaths quickened and she looked uncomfortable in her own skin. It was sudden, starting once we'd come to Florence, a new behavior she'd never shown before.

I liked it.

I moved into her, my arms circling around her small frame, engulfed in the smell of roses. With my eyes locked to hers, I watched her swallow, watched her eyes drop momentarily because the stare was too much.

My hand slid up the back of her neck and into her thick hair, pulling it from her face slightly as I forced her eyes on me. My thumb supported her chin, just an inch from those beautiful lips. "You're afraid of me."

With nowhere to go, she shifted her eyes back and forth between mine, her breaths noticeable against my palm at her back. The silence stretched for eternity, her frame stiff in my embrace. "In so many words…"

Good. "I'm a dangerous man, but I'm no danger to you."

Her eyes continued to flick back and forth, silently argumentative.

My hand slid to her throat, and I held on as I kissed her. Our lips came together instantly, and I felt the breath release from her lungs in relief. She was suddenly soft in my arms, like a warm cloud that would float to the sky if I didn't keep my grasp. My arm tightened on the small of her back as I pulled her flush to me, feeling the lace from her bra against my bare skin. The smell of roses got stronger, like I was standing in a summer garden.

The heat was searing like it always was, like a piece of raw meat in a sizzling-hot pan. I could feel the smoke between our mouths. My hand reached for her back, and I unclasped the bra. Straps came loose. The material stopped hugging her body. I gripped it and yanked it off, finally feeling her bare flesh against mine. Her nipples were hard as if she was cold. I squeezed her against me again, feeling her take a breath and release a moan so quiet I wasn't sure if I heard it.

I dragged her thong off next, getting the tiny material off that gorgeous ass. My hand grabbed one cheek and squeezed it firmly, my dick so hard in my shorts it hurt.

Her little hands reached for my bottoms and pushed them off my hips so my cock could come free. Now her confidence returned, her nails dug into me, her eyes reflecting the arousal in my gaze.

Her naked body was indescribable. With nice tits, womanly hips, a mouth perfect for sucking dick, she boiled my fucking brain. I'd wanted to fuck her a moment ago, but now I wanted her to fuck me instead. I pushed down on her shoulder, guiding her to her knees in front of me.

She obeyed, her knees folding underneath her body.

I grabbed her throat and shoved myself inside, so desperate to get that lipstick all over my dick. I didn't even give her a chance to breathe before I burrowed myself deep inside. I slid across that slick tongue and made myself right at home. With my hand gripping the back of her neck, I went to town. I watched the tears pool in her eyes. Watched the saliva drip from the corners of her mouth like rain falling off the corners of a roof after a storm. Watched her keep up with my demands to get me off.

I gripped the back of her hair as I finished, giving her my entire length as I watched her struggle not to choke. I filled her throat as I watched her writhe while she held her breath, doing her best to keep it together until I was finished.

I finally let her go, and she instantly gasped for breath.

"Come on, sweetheart." I grabbed her by the arm and helped her up. "We aren't done yet." I got her on the edge of the bed and lowered myself to my knees. My face moved between her thighs, and I kissed the wet pussy waiting for me.

Her body gave an involuntary jerk when she felt me. Then the moan followed. It was like the growl of a bear that had finally gotten the honey. Her fingers dug into my hair, and she ground her hips against me, immediately falling into the pleasure my mouth gave her. "Bartholomew…"

When she said my name like that, I could do this all night.

17

LAURA

The butler escorted me to the drawing room, the same room where I'd stabbed Lucas with that burning cigar. Most of my childhood memories of my father took place in this room. In the winter, the fireplace had burning logs. In the summer, the curtains were drawn shut in the afternoons to keep out the sun.

Today, the curtains were open, and there was no fire.

My father sat in the armchair, a drink beside him, his cigar smashed in the ashtray but the room smelling like a cloud of smoke as if he'd put it out right before I got there. He looked at me, his anger barely suppressed behind that furious gaze.

I took a seat in the other armchair, keeping the table between us. My father had never struck me, but I wasn't sure what he was capable of anymore. I crossed my legs and stared, my fingers curling into a fist underneath my chin.

"I want a name, Laura."

"So, no small talk, then?" I asked. "Not even a comment about the weather?"

Now he looked even more pissed off. "I'll find him whether you tell me or not. And when I do, I'll break both his legs and throw them in my goddamn fireplace—"

"Touch him, and I'll burn your eyes out with your cigars." I'd used my inside voice a moment ago, but I exploded like a volcano once I heard his threat. "How about that? You aren't the only one who can make threats, Leonardo." He was still a strong man, but without a weapon, I could slam my chair over his head and knock him out cold. Growing up as the daughter of the Skull King had taught me a few things. I was sure he hadn't forgotten. "Lucas tried to throw a punch, and my man—" I hesitated when I described him that way, because it felt so right to say "—my man defended me. I'm not sorry for what happened, and as a father, you should be relieved that your daughter's boyfriend isn't afraid to get his hands dirty once in a while."

"You're my daughter now?" he asked coldly. "Because you called me Leonardo two seconds ago."

I held his stare and let the silence pass. "Lucas will make a full recovery. Let's move on."

"Move on? I'm in the midst of a crisis."

"Then you don't have time to worry about my boyfriend, do you?"

He sank into the armchair, and once his fingers tapped the wood of the armrest, I knew he was really furious.

"As long as that asshole Lucas doesn't touch me again, we'll have no more problems. So, let it go."

His fingers continued to drum. *Tap. Tap. Tap.*

"My man finished it, but yours started it. Remember that."

His fingers tapped for a long time, his unblinking eyes focused on me across the room. Seconds continued, turning into a full minute. It got so quiet that the cars were audible outside the front gate. "It's ironic, don't you think?"

What?

"You run off to Paris because you want nothing to do with this life. Because you're ashamed of what I do. Ashamed of what I've built. Ashamed of everything I've done to give you the life of a princess. And yet, here you are, in bed with someone just like me."

"He's not like you."

"He couldn't have hurt Lucas like that unless he knew what he was doing. I don't need to know much about him to know we're cut from the same cloth, to know he's me, just thirty years younger."

I could feel the pulse in my neck. Like a drum.

"You accept him, but not me?" He tempered his voice, letting it grow quiet in volume but loud in emotion. "It's okay for him to kill people, but not me? Is he an arms dealer? Is he a trafficker? Those things are okay, but drugs are off-limits?"

My eyes shifted to the window.

"As much as it hurt me, I understood your decision to walk away. But now, I think you're just a hypocrite."

I looked at him again. "He's *not* like you. He wouldn't let me get raped. He wouldn't let me be murdered." He had the grace to blink, to shift his gaze away when I reminded him of his unforgivable mistake. "When someone crosses me, he protects me. Your son-in-law gave your daughter a black eye, and you behave like it's nothing. Your son-in-law tried to punch me, and it's inconsequential to you. No, you're *nothing* alike."

"Victor stopped it—"

"*You* should have stopped it. How can I stay here when I know you won't protect me? It's open season, and I've got a fucking target on my back."

He looked away completely.

"He's not the man I'll marry, but he's the one I need right now. If you don't want to deal with him again, then don't fuck with me." I rose to my feet and prepared to walk out. "Those are words I should be able to say about you… but I can't."

"Laura."

I'd just stepped out of the double doors when I heard his voice from behind me. I pretended I hadn't heard him and continued forward.

"Laura."

I stopped and gave a loud sigh. "Yes?"

Victor appeared at my side. In a short-sleeved shirt and dark jeans, he didn't look cold despite the springtime chill. There'd been more showers than sunshine this year. His eyes quickly took me in and assessed my unease. "Let's get a coffee."

"Why?" I blurted.

He looked slightly taken aback. "I'd like to talk to you, and I can tell you don't want to be here a moment longer than you have to."

I headed out the iron gates that separated the property from the public street. "Fine."

In silence, we walked a couple blocks until we stopped at the first café we could find. I ordered an Americano when I'd prefer alcohol, and he got the same thing. Because I wanted some comfort food, I grabbed a muffin too.

We sat together at a small table, the café empty because it was afternoon and everyone was having lunch. Victor sat there, his eyes on me nearly the entire time, looking at me like I was a bomb that might go off if he touched the wrong wire.

I picked at the poppy seed muffin, sticking to the top because that was the best part.

"You still do that?"

I grabbed a small chunk and put it in my mouth as I looked at him. "What?"

"You only eat the top."

"Well, the rest of it sucks."

He showed a small glimmer of a smile.

"What did you want to talk about, Victor?" I needed to return to Paris. I had clients who needed their clothes, and I knew Bartholomew needed to get back so he could...do whatever he did in the middle of the night.

"How'd the conversation go with your father?"

"Like all the rest. Shitty."

"For what it's worth, I think Lucas deserved what he got."

I picked off another piece as I looked at him.

"I should have done it myself."

"You don't like him?"

"Now I don't," he said. "I didn't know he was hurting your sister."

I had been prepared to punch Victor in the face when I saw him again, but I realized he wasn't a bad guy. We were both young, and he made some mistakes. He wasn't an asshole like Lucas. "I'm gonna try to talk some sense into her. Maybe after the fiftieth try, she'll listen."

"Yeah, maybe," he said noncommittally.

I drank my coffee and took a few more bites of my muffin.

He took a drink before he cleared his throat. "I also wanted to talk to you about that guy you're seeing."

"What about him?"

"I can tell he's been in the game for a long time."

He'd been in the game since birth.

"Not the kind of guy you fuck with."

Nope.

"Not sure if he's the kind of guy you should be involved with."

"Really?" I asked with a half laugh. "That's rich, coming from you."

"Just looking out for you, is all."

"Victor, I needed you to look out for me seven years ago. Not now."

His eyes flicked away from my attack. "We deal with a lot of assholes in this line of business. Lot of cronies. Lot of muscle. I'm not sure who he works for or what kind of business he's in—"

"He's the boss," I snapped. "He doesn't work for anyone." The pride in my voice surprised even me—the one who said it.

Victor stared for a while before he gave a nod. "All the more reason to stay away from him."

"I can take care of myself, Victor."

"He's dangerous—"

"To you. But I've got nothing to worry about."

He looked out the window, his steaming cup of coffee sitting in the saucer in front of him. "I've thought about you a lot over these last seven years. More than guilt. More than remorse. I thought about what could have been if I'd talked to someone…or we'd gotten help…if we'd stayed—"

"If *you'd* stayed, you mean."

He turned to look at me. "Yeah…if I'd stayed. What would have been. Because you know I loved you, Laura. I meant it the first time I said it. I meant it the day we got married. I still meant it when I asked for a divorce."

"Don't dwell on the things you can't change, Victor."

He stared at me head on, his eyes looking the way they did seven years ago. "You think you'd ever give me another chance?" His voice was quiet, like he was already braced for the ferocity of my response.

"Why would I?"

"Because you loved me too."

I did. But that was a long time ago. When I was a different person. When I was under my father's thumb like a child. "He hunted down all four of the men who did that to me…and killed every last one of them. I didn't even have to ask. He just did it."

He looked down at the table.

"You had seven years to do the same—and you were my husband."

"It's complicated—"

"It's not that complicated. Not complicated at all."

"Your father made a truce with them—"

"Wow…he's even more vile than I realized." *You didn't make a truce with your daughter's rapist. You didn't make peace with the men who killed your wife.* I always thought he was the ultimate asshole, but now I wondered if he was the ultimate coward.

"I had no way to get their names—"

"Well, my man got them."

He looked at me again. "Because he's dangerous, like I said."

"Because he puts his money where his mouth is. Because he gets shit done. Because he's a *man*."

He gave a brief cringe like those words actually wounded him.

"You have a lot of balls, asking me for another chance."

"I knew I'd regret it if I didn't."

"Especially when you know I have a boyfriend."

"I know that's a short-term thing."

"Why would you assume that?" My arms folded on the table.

"Because men like that don't settle down."

He was right on the money.

"And I know he's not the kind of husband you want anyway."

"And you think you are?" I asked incredulously.

"You married me once, didn't you?"

"I was young and stupid—"

"And you loved me." He grew more confident, more like the man I remembered. "You're getting older—"

"Don't clock my ovaries. That's not going to work."

"I'm just saying we want the same things—"

"I want a man who stays by my side through sickness and health. Not someone who takes off the second shit gets hard—"

"I learned my lesson. I would never do anything like that again."

"Oh good," I snapped. "I'm glad you finally got your shit together. Yes, let's pick up right where we left off." I rolled my eyes and crossed my arms over my chest. "So fucking romantic. *Baby, I'm okay with you being raped now. Let's make some babies...*"

He closed his eyes as he cringed. "This is not how I wanted this conversation to go—"

"This conversation shouldn't have happened in the first place. You had your chance, and you blew it, Victor."

"Look, I'm willing to leave the business behind to start over with you. If you want to live in Paris, that's fine with me. If you want to move to Greece, I don't care. I don't give a damn where we live—"

"Never going to happen, Victor. Accept my answer."

He looked away, giving a quiet sigh in irritation. "So, you'll date a kingpin, a guy who's done unspeakable things, but my actions are simply unforgivable?"

"You were my husband, Victor."

"And I was young. And stupid. Forgive me."

"Victor—"

"Forgive me."

"I'm not obligated to sacrifice my feelings for yours. You think you've suffered? It's nothing compared to what I've been through. Nothing compared to the years of therapy that cost me a small fortune."

He looked away again, and when the light hit his eyes, it showed the shine on the surface. It showed the small pool that had formed there, the pain that he kept below the surface. He blinked, and it vanished like it'd never been there.

"But I forgive you." The words tumbled out on their own. To my surprise, I actually felt better, felt lighter.

He looked at me, and his eyes were still in shock. He didn't blink. Didn't take a breath. "Thank you."

When I returned to the house, Bartholomew was in his office. I could tell he was on the phone because his deep voice drifted down the hallway, and his tone was serious, like he was taking care of business.

I grabbed my things and started to pack.

He walked in moments later, in nothing but dark sweatpants that hung low on his hips, looking hot as fuck as usual. His beard was already coming in even though he'd just shaved. It was a shadow, but in another day, his entire chin would be covered. He looked at me in his special way, in a way that other men had tried to recreate but could only poorly imitate. His gaze was powerful, commanding my body without saying a single word. His eyes bored into mine as he drew close, asking me questions that he never spoke.

"I smoothed everything over."

He continued to stare.

"Just steer clear of him and his men."

"That shouldn't be a problem—as long as they don't touch my woman." He walked to the bar and poured himself a drink, his muscular back to me, oblivious to the way my legs had just softened into jelly. He tilted his head back and took a big drink before he wiped his mouth on the back of his forearm. "You were gone a long time."

My heart stiffened in my chest. Everything stiffened.

He looked at me when I didn't say anything.

"Victor asked me to coffee."

His stare was hard as stone, his thoughts impossible to decipher. "What did he want?"

"To check on me, I guess."

"And he thinks that's his responsibility because…?" His tone didn't change, but that stare was unsettling.

"He knows my relationship with my father is tense."

He approached me, his bare feet on the hardwood then the rug surrounding the bed. He grew taller the closer he came, and then he cast me in his shadow. "I don't need another man checking on my woman. Should I tell him that myself, or would you like to handle it?"

Jesus. It was like he'd been there in the coffee shop and overheard the entire thing. "I'll relay the message."

"Good." He walked back to the bar, grabbed his drink, and took a seat on the couch. "What else did he say?"

Shit, like I'd ever tell. "Said that you were dangerous and I should be careful."

A half smile moved on to his hard face. "Only half of that sentence is true." He grabbed the glass and took another drink before he licked his lips. "He should take his own advice if he doesn't want to eat my gun."

I moved to the other couch, keeping my distance from his silent hostility. "Don't you think you're overreacting?"

The second his eyes shifted to my face, I knew I'd said the wrong thing.

"*Overreacting.*" He said the word like it was a brand-new addition to his vocabulary. He was testing the word on his tongue, like no one else had ever been stupid enough to describe him that way. "There's a side of me that you've never seen, sweetheart. A side that does overreact. Trust me, I'm not overreacting now." His fingers curled into a fist and rested against his cheek while his ankle rested on the opposite knee. "I don't appreciate a man sniffing around a woman who clearly belongs to me, especially when he's a pussy-ass bitch who already failed you. He gets a warning this time, but next time, his lips will be sealed around the barrel of my gun like it's a cock in his mouth."

I felt the tremble down my spine, felt the fear that everyone else felt when they were around him. The danger that Victor warned me about...it was looking me in the face. "I never said Victor came on to me—"

"You didn't need to. I'm a lot smarter than you realize, Laura."

"And even if he did, what does it matter—"

"It *matters* because you're mine." He still didn't raise his voice. Didn't throw his arms down in a rage. But his control over his emotions was more terrifying than the combustion of those emotions. He could convey so much with so little. Could scream at the top of his lungs with just a whisper. "And he knows that. He knew it when you told him I was your hot-as-fuck boyfriend. Knew it when I stabbed Lucas. Knew it when you told him I killed those motherfuckers. He knows what happens when you disrespect men like me, but he seems to have forgotten."

"Wait...how did you know I told him that?"

"Because I knew you would. He needed to know I did what he should have done seven years ago. And you wanted him to know that too." He reached for his glass and finished the contents. Then unexpectedly, he threw the glass at the wall, and it shattered into pieces. "Make sure he knows you're the only reason he's alive right now."

Somehow, like always, we ended up in bed.

He pinned my face to the mattress with my ass in the air, the arch in my back so prominent it hurt a little, and pounded into me like I was a woman he'd spotted across the bar and took home for the night.

I took that big dick over and over, panting into the sheets balled near my face, knowing he was conquering my land and claiming it as his all over again. His fingers fisted my hair as he kept me in place, his other hand gripping my hip as he pushed harder and harder, driving me into an orgasm and then the next…over and over.

When he was finally finished, he let me go.

He lay back on the pillow, one arm tucked under his head, his body shiny with sweat.

I straightened my back and felt the discomfort subside before I lay flat on my stomach, catching my breath even though he was the one who'd done all the work. We lay there in silence, and I was so satisfied and comfortable I could fall asleep, even though it was the middle of the day.

"What happened with your father?"

I sat up and ran my fingers through my hair. "You know, he made some threats... I made some of my own."

He sat up against the headboard and looked at me.

"Basically said I was a hypocrite for being with someone like you."

He turned his stare straight ahead and looked outside.

"But I told him you were nothing alike. He's never protected me, but you do."

His eyes were back on me, impossible to read.

"He and I...we're never going to get along."

"There's no reason you have to."

"Really?" I asked. "Even though he's my father?"

"Tolerating someone you hate is toxic to your sanity. Family is no exception."

"Yeah..." I sat up farther and grabbed his shirt at the edge of the bed. I pulled it on, cold from the draft that came from the terrace. "But I've got to help my sister. She's too young to know better."

He watched me run my fingers through my hair. "I need to get back. Have business that requires my attention."

"I do too. I'm behind on work."

"Then we'll leave tonight."

"I'll have to come back and deal with my sister later."

"I'll come with you. And if I can't, you're still welcome to stay here."

I couldn't turn down an offer like that. A beautiful home right in the heart of Florence. My favorite gelato place was so close. And his clothes were in the closet, so I could wear one of his shirts to bed. "Thanks."

18

BARTHOLOMEW

I sat in the parlor, Bleu on the couch across from me, the rest of my men sprinkled throughout the room, listening to the conversation with attentive ears.

"The Moroccans have cut ties with Leonardo," Bleu said. "Naturally, Leonardo is in full-on meltdown."

Now that I knew how he treated his daughter, this was even more satisfying. "Good." I brought the cigar to my lips and took a deep puff, my body humming with power. "And he's got one man down too." That was just the icing on the cake.

"He'll turn to different partnerships in his desperation. Probably even the US."

"But we know that won't go anywhere." I rested my arm on the armrest, grinning like a fool. I'd moved my chess pieces and had my checkmate before Leonardo even realized we were playing. The death of his brother couldn't have been more convenient. Too distracted by the funeral and revenge against his small-time enemies, he had no idea that a much bigger shark had joined the bloody waters.

"No."

"Good work, Bleu." I stabbed my cigar into the ashtray before I stood up.

"Are you leaving?"

"Yes." I headed to my bedroom to change. "The prime minister is expecting me."

I parked at the curb and walked to the front door. The lights in the window were on, so I knew she was in residence. My hands straightened my obnoxious suit jacket before I walked up the stone steps.

The door opened—and it was Cauldron. "Bartholomew."

I gave a slight nod. "Is she ready?"

"Trying to fit into her dress."

It was an odd thing to say, so I gave him a stare.

"She's pregnant."

Great.

"She's not showing yet. But in another month or two, it'll be an issue." He opened the door wider so I could enter the townhouse.

My eyes swept the room as I looked for her. The downstairs was empty.

"This is the part where you say congratulations."

I turned to look at him, my hands sliding into my pockets. "I guess we have different definitions of accomplishment."

Cauldron held my gaze, wearing sweatpants and a t-shirt like he intended to sit on the couch until she came home.

"Is this something you even want?" I asked. "Or something *she* wants?"

Cauldron considered his response before he spoke. "I have my reservations. But if I'm going to do this with anyone, it's her."

"Your life is going to be piss for the next twenty years."

He stared. "Had a bad childhood?"

I looked away and ignored the question.

"You can't have the good without the bad. You'll never have a son stand at your height unless you hold him in your arms first."

"You know what I don't like about kids? They grow up to be people—and I hate people."

Camille came down the stairs at that moment, wearing a black cocktail dress that hid her small stomach. She had her clutch under her arm, her thick hair in shiny curls. She only had eyes for Cauldron as she said goodbye. "I'll see you in a couple of hours."

He kissed her and let her go. Then he looked at me. "I don't see how this is going to work in a couple months."

"Figure it out—because you made a deal."

Camille sat beside me at the table. Dinner had already been served, and the plates were being cleared. There was a crowd around the prime minister, and my opportunity hadn't arrived yet.

Her hand went to her stomach under the table. "I'm not sure if Cauldron told you—"

"He did."

"We started trying, but we didn't think it would happen so quickly."

My eyes were focused across the room, watching the way the prime minister's wife sat there in silence because no one was interested in speaking to her. Camille couldn't distract her because she wasn't even part of the conversation.

"I'm so excited."

Was she still going on about it?

"Is there something wrong, Bartholomew?"

"No." I kept my gaze focused.

"You just seem more...angry than usual."

"I guess I'm a little tired of all the pregnancy talk." Maybe that would shut her up.

She turned quiet.

Thank God.

"I thought you would be happy for us."

"I'm not the kind of guy who's happy for other people."

"Because you aren't happy for yourself?" she snapped.

A little smile moved on to my lips. "Guess you could say that."

"You don't ever think about the future? Ever think about settling down—"

"No."

"There's more to life than money—"

"Only poor people say that."

"Well, I'm not poor."

"But you were." My eyes remained focused, trying to figure out an opening for a conversation.

"Alright, enough of the baby talk."

I grabbed my glass and took a drink. It was white wine—far too sweet for my taste.

"How are things with you?"

"We don't have to talk."

"See?" she said. "You're angrier than usual."

"Not angry. Just have a lot on my mind."

"Like?"

"I'm about to take Italy. Begin my distribution there. Make the Skull King my bitch."

"The Skull King?"

"Not important."

"Well, you should get laid during all this ambition because you're tense."

"I am." I hadn't seen Laura since we'd returned to Paris. We both had shit that required our attention, work that we had to catch up on. It'd been five days since I'd had those tits in my mouth, and I was definitely starting to miss it. Every time I got a waft of roses, my dick got hard.

"Well, the whores aren't working because you're still an ass."

"She's not a whore."

"*She?*" Both of her eyebrows rose at that bit of information. "That sounds singular."

I'd said too much.

"Do you…have a girlfriend?" She said the words with utter shock, like she couldn't believe someone like me could be monogamous.

It was a fair assumption, I supposed.

"Holy shit, *you* have a girlfriend?"

"That's not how I would describe it."

"Alright, then how would you describe it?"

"She's my woman." I kept my eyes across the room, dividing my attention between two different things.

"Isn't that the same thing?"

"Not in the slightest. A teenage boy can have a girlfriend. I have a grown-ass woman."

"This sounds serious."

"No."

"*My woman* sounds pretty possessive."

"Because I am possessive. I'm possessive toward all things that belong to me. My money. My cars. My homes. She's just another item on the list."

"How long has this been going on?"

"Little over a month."

"Then this relationship is moving fast."

Since nothing was happening with the prime minister, I looked at her. "We started at a high speed—and it's remained that way ever since."

"Bartholomew, you're going to have to change your perspective on kids if you want this to go anywhere."

"I don't want it to go anywhere. Neither does she."

"So...it's just a fling?"

Not how I would describe it. "I guess you can say that."

"Do you do those a lot?"

"Not really. Laura is one of the few."

"Laura...pretty name."

The conversation finally died, and we sat in silence. The men with the prime minister finally moved on. My opportunity would arrive shortly.

"I just don't understand how you can call her your woman but say you don't want anything more." Of course, the conversation wasn't over for Camille. She had to poke and prod.

"I want all the benefits of an intense relationship without all the bullshit. That's how."

"You aren't afraid you're going to get hurt?"

"No." Not in the slightest. Couldn't remember the last time anything hurt me.

"Well, aren't you worried about her getting hurt?"

"No. Like I said, she's a grown-ass woman. She can take care of herself."

Camille stared, her eyes shifting back and forth between mine.

"Are we done with this conversation?"

She gave a nod. "Yeah."

When I entered my home, my butler immediately looked at my hands.

They were covered in blood.

But like the good servant he was, he didn't say a word.

I headed straight to the bathroom and scrubbed all the blood from my hands and underneath my fingernails. The white basin turned pink with the stains. I had to keep scrubbing, keep applying soap, until my hands were finally what they used to be. I wiped them clean then looked at my knuckles.

Still bloody.

I entered the hallway. "Gauze."

"I have everything ready for you, sir." My butler stood at the kitchen island with the first aid kit spread out. The alcohol and swabs were there, along with the stitch kit and everything else.

I poured the alcohol over my hands right on the counter.

He didn't give a reaction whatsoever.

I patted them dry then wrapped them both in gauze.

"Ice, sir?"

"No." I left everything on the counter and headed to my bedroom on the next floor. As I went up the stairs, I looked out the window and saw that it was almost dawn. Sunlight penetrated the very edge of the horizon as a hazy pink.

I dropped my clothes then looked at my knuckles.

They'd already bled through.

Whatever.

I closed all the curtains and plunged my bedroom into utter darkness before I got into bed. Just when I lay down, my phone lit up on my nightstand.

I reached for it and felt the blue light hit my face.

I want to see you.

She didn't beat around the bush or fish for my attention. Felt no resentment because I hadn't texted her in nearly a week. She felt no expectation toward me whatsoever. That was the difference between a girl and a woman. *I'll come over tonight.*

That's a long time from now...

I've had a long night, sweetheart.

What if I come to you?

That was an offer I couldn't refuse. *My butler will escort you to my room.*

See you soon.

I texted my butler then fell asleep right away.

I woke up again when I heard the door open and close. Footsteps approached the bed. Clothes hit the rug. Then a beautiful woman tugged the blankets off and climbed up my body. Her lips kissed my chest and my stomach, making their way down until they sealed around my hard length and gave me a wet kiss.

It was so dark I could barely see anything, but I knew that mouth like my own hand. She sucked my dick, ran her tongue over my balls, made me harder than I'd ever been in my life, and then sat on top of me and sank.

Fuck...this pussy.

My hands squeezed her tits as she ground her hips, handling my big dick the way only a real woman could. My hands went to her ass next, wanting to touch all of her at once. The pain in my knuckles was forgotten, even though I made them bleed more every time I gripped her. The need to fuck her like a savage overcame me, and I rolled her to her back and moved over her before I pounded her into the sheets, her head right against the headboard. She was folded underneath me like a pretzel, my hand hooked into her hair like bait on a hook.

I fucked her so hard she screamed when she came. Her nails sliced into my arms and my back. It was too dark to see her tears, but I could hear them in the break of her voice. My hips between her soft thighs, I came with a victorious moan, feeling like a king every time I fucked this sexy-as-hell woman.

We breathed together, still tangled up just like the sheets.

"I thought you'd had a long night?" Her thighs squeezed my hips, my dick still inside her, our come mixed together.

I could have just lain there and enjoyed the fruit of her labor, but we were like a burning match and gasoline. My fuse was lit, and I had to move as fast as possible, like a drill breaking through rock, getting as deep as I could go. "Not long enough."

Instead of going to bed, I had breakfast sent to my bedroom. The curtains were open, and we sat together at the dining table in my living area. My exhaustion wasn't enough to ask her to leave.

The first thing she noticed was my hands.

"Shit...what happened?" She grabbed my left hand and examined the blood soaked into the gauze.

"Not as bad as it looks."

"Well, that's still pretty bad because this looks horrendous."

I pulled my hand away, letting it rest on my thigh underneath the table.

"Bartholomew—"

"You're making it a bigger deal than it needs to be. I've broken and bloodied these knuckles more times than I can count." I grabbed my fork and took a bite of my steak. Steak and egg whites, my usual breakfast—or dinner, I should say.

"Why don't you just use a gun like everyone else?"

I took my time chewing my bite, choosing my words carefully. "Anyone can shoot someone. But not everyone can beat a man to death. Gets the message across more effectively. Word spreads on the street. I'm not the kind of man you fuck with."

When she realized I'd killed a man before I'd come home and fucked her, her rosy cheeks suddenly became pale. Her eyes dropped to her food as the understanding pierced through her skin and sank into her bones.

Maybe I shouldn't have told her. "Don't ask for answers you can't handle."

"Who said I can't handle it?" she asked quietly.

"You're the color of my sheets."

She added more cream to her coffee before she took a drink. "Who are you killing? Men who have betrayed you?"

"You really want to go there?"

"Would I have asked otherwise?" She lifted her gaze and looked at me. Her eyes were hard as steel, but the rest of her face showed her unease at my barbarism.

"My men don't betray me. They're paid well. They're treated well. Unlike other kingpins, I think you have to give respect to earn it. The men who suffer my wrath are those who think they can shave pennies off the dollar."

She looked at me like she didn't know what that meant.

"Some of my distributors try to pocket more than their share…like I won't notice. But I have spies everywhere. For an enterprise this big, I need eyes everywhere, watching every little thing people do. Whether it's a thousand euros or a single dollar, the punishment is the same. I beat them to death with my bare hands, stomp on their skulls with my boots until they crack, or turn their body into chum with a metal bat."

She held the coffee mug in her hand, still and silent, like a deer in the headlights on a winter night.

"We don't have to continue this conversation." She was tougher than most women, probably because of the things she'd seen growing up, probably because she'd watched her mother die and survived her own trauma. But it still disturbed her.

"Aren't you worried that someone is going to want revenge?"

"A lot of people do."

"And you just...don't let it bother you?"

"A wolf doesn't concern himself with the thoughts of sheep, right?"

"No, but arrogance like that can get you killed."

A small smile moved on to my lips. "You worried about me, sweetheart?"

She drank from her cup.

"I own most of the buildings around me. Security is stationed there twenty-four hours a day, searching for snipers, surveilling anyone who comes within a few blocks. I have men deep undercover with my enemies as well as my allies. I'm here, there, everywhere all at once."

She swallowed before she returned her cup to the table. "That sounds exhausting."

"I find it thrilling."

"So...do you have men watching me? Making sure I'm not a spy for someone else? That I'm not going to slit your throat while you sleep and betray you?"

I held her gaze, seeing the way her eyes were guarded in anticipation of my answer.

"I have men watch you—but only to keep you safe."

"Really?" she whispered.

"Yes."

"Why? Why am I different from everyone else?"

Now I was cornered into giving an answer I didn't want to share. This conversation had made her as white as snow, but now it made my hands turn cold despite the heat from my injury. I was stiff but loose at the same time, looking into eyes that sparkled more than a pile of diamonds. "Because this is real."

"Who was it this time?" Benton addressed my hands without looking at them.

"Andre." I took a drink.

He sat across from me at the table in the bar. It was ten in the evening, so most of the seats were empty. Benton had a sleepiness to his gaze, like he wasn't used to staying up late these days. "Didn't expect that."

"Neither did I."

"That must have been hard for you."

"Not really." Betray me—and you were dead to me.

"How did you find out?"

"One of the guys did a deep dive into their records because he suspected Andre was skimming off the top. I didn't believe it since Andre isn't the stupid type, but it turned out to be true."

"You're certain of that?"

"He admitted it before I killed him."

Benton took a drink then licked his lips. "Fuck me."

Andre had taken the hits like a man. Didn't beg. Didn't plead. Didn't make a sound. I respected him—even as I took his life. "It is what it is." I took a drink and left the empty glass on the table.

"You're awfully calm about this."

Now I was. "Even the most honorable men can't resist temptation when it's right in front of them. Whether it's cheating on their wife with a woman half her age, or adjusting the scales and pocketing some change. The love of their life could leave them. Or they could lose their life. But in the moment, it all seems worth it." I waved the waitress over, and she immediately brought me another drink. "They always think they can outsmart me—fucking hilarious." I released a quick chuckle before I took a drink. "How's the wife?"

Benton took a while to answer, like he was thinking about his time at my side. "Uncomfortable. She's a petite woman, so pregnancy doesn't agree with her."

"No surprise there."

"We're thinking of moving to my place in the countryside. Outgrowing the townhouse."

"Claire will have to change schools."

"She makes friends easily."

"How is she?" I asked.

Benton grew quiet again. "There are moments when her eyes glaze over, like she's thinking about it...or her mother. But for the most part, she's the same happy girl she's always been." He took a drink, the ice cubes rushing to his lips before he set the glass down again. "Bleu?"

"He's really proven himself."

Benton stared at me, his hard expression hiding the anger underneath.

"What do you want me to do, Benton? Fire him?"

He stared at his glass.

"Remember, he came to me."

"Trust me, I know." He took another drink.

"He didn't want to build apartments anymore. He wanted to make some real money—"

"At what cost?" Benton snapped. "Pushing drugs on the street? He already saw what I went through."

"What did you go through *exactly*?" I said coldly. "Your townhouse is worth over two million euros, and your estate outside the city is worth ten million. The only reason you can put Claire in private school and have your wife be a housewife is because of me."

Benton was dead silent for seconds, and that was basically the same thing as screaming. "Are we going to pretend you didn't take Claire—"

"That was after—"

"If I didn't do what you wanted, you were going to make me do it anyway. Like I was your goddamn slave." His face turned red.

"I apologized for that—"

"And I'll never forgive you."

It was like a little knife in my side. Didn't see it coming. "If you want me to get rid of Bleu, I will. I'll take the blame. He'll never have to know that you asked."

Benton remained quiet, apparently too angry to speak.

I remained still, holding his gaze without blinking.

"No."

"No, what?"

"I won't interfere with his life decisions. If I did, I would be no better than you."

"You shot me, remember? I thought we were past this."

"My daughter was imprisoned by a bunch of acid-pushing freaks. No, we'll never be past this, Bartholomew." He finished the rest of his glass then walked straight out of the bar—without looking back.

When are you coming?

I'd forgotten about our plans. *I'm not. Shit came up.*

Everything okay?

Everything is fucking great.

Can I call you?

I ignored the question. I left the phone on the desk as I sat there, a bottle and a glass in front of me, ignoring all the work that required my attention because I was too furious to focus.

The phone rang, and her name appeared.

I ignored it, dragging my fingers over the coarse hair along my jawline.

She didn't leave a message.

But she called me again. It kept vibrating on the desk with every ring.

Bleu walked into the room. "The car will be here in five minutes."

All I had to do was give him a look, and that changed our plans.

"Let us know when you're ready." He shut the door behind him.

I grabbed the phone and answered. "What?"

"I—I just wanted to know if you're okay."

"I told you I was fine."

"But you clearly aren't fine."

Silence. Seething silence.

"You can always talk to me. I want you to know that."

"Message received." I hung up on her.

She didn't call back.

19

LAURA

Knock. Knock. Knock.

I sat at the small dining table as I worked on my laptop, a glass of red wine beside me. My eyes flicked to the entryway and the shadow under the door. It was past eight in the evening, and only one person stopped by unexpectedly whenever he felt like it.

I opened the door and gave him a cold stare.

In his leather jacket, black jeans, and thick boots, he looked like he was born out of darkness. His arms hung at his sides, and he stared at me with eyes so dark they looked like bullets.

My hand remained on the door. "What's the magic word?"

His eyes were still as they burned into my face. He didn't seem to breathe, didn't seem to move at all. Sometimes the only way I knew he was alive was when my hand rested on his chest and felt his heartbeat. "I'm sorry."

That was easier than I expected. My hand dropped from the door, and I returned to my chair at the dining table.

He shut the door and followed me to the table, taking a seat across from me, a man far too big for my cheap little chairs. His knees were wide apart, and his hands rested together in his lap.

I closed my computer then tucked my legs against my body. I was in little pajama shorts and a cotton sweater that left one shoulder bare. My makeup was long gone because I hadn't expected my lover to stop by after the way he'd behaved. That was yesterday, and I hadn't heard from him since.

He hadn't taken his eyes off me. "You're still angry."

"Yep." I grabbed the wine and took a drink.

"I apologized."

"Doesn't mean I'm ready to accept that apology."

His eyes dropped momentarily. "You shouldn't have called me."

"I was worried—"

"Don't ever worry about me." His eyes were back on mine, commanding.

"That's like asking me not to care about you. Impossible to do."

He turned quiet, just watching me. "In case this isn't obvious, I'm not the kind of man that *talks*. I don't control or temper my emotions. I scream. I yell. And I kill people. That's how I express myself. So, when I'm angry—stay the fuck away from me."

"You control your emotions with me."

"You've never seen me angry."

"I don't know… You seemed pretty angry about Victor."

He went quiet again, crafting his response in silence. "If I behaved the way I wanted to behave, this would be over. I had no other option but to remain calm."

"You could have remained calm when I called. I just wanted to talk to you—"

"And I didn't want to talk to you."

"Then why did you answer?"

"Because if I didn't, you would worry."

I drank from my wine again. Didn't bother to offer him any. "What made you so upset?"

There was a flash of anger across his face. "I told you I don't talk."

"But you do talk. You've told me about your parents, about the woman who made the biggest mistake of her life by leaving you, and the fact that you killed some asshole with your bare hands. You do talk, Bartholomew."

He looked away slightly and released a chuckle. "Biggest mistake of her life..."

"What?"

He released a quiet scoff. "Nothing."

I stared at the side of his face and waited for him to say something more, but he didn't. "Point is, you share your life with me. Why is this any different?"

He looked at me again.

"Talk to me."

He released a quiet sigh. "You really want to know?"

"Yes."

"I must warn you—I'm the villain in this tale."

Goose bumps formed on my arms.

"You aren't going to want to fuck me anymore after I tell you."

"You still wanted to fuck me after I told you I was raped."

"Not the same thing, sweetheart," he said. "At all." He watched me across the table, observing the features of my face.

"I can handle it."

"We'll see about that." He left the chair and helped himself to my kitchen, pouring himself a glass of wine before he took a seat. "I told you I have one friend. Benton."

"Yes, I remember."

"And I told you that I helped him get his daughter back from the acid-dealing freaks at the camp."

"Yes."

"Well, I left out one small detail..." He took a drink before he set down the glass. "I was the one who put her there in the first place." His fingers rested on the stem of his glass as he looked at me, waiting for my reaction.

It took a few seconds for me to understand the implication of his words. "Why-why would you do that?"

"It was the only way I could get Benton back. The original plan was for his ex to be taken, the mother of his daughter. He had no affection for her, but I knew he would do anything to get her back for his daughter. I knew he would ask me to help him get Beatrice back—and in return—I would demand his servitude. But unfortunately, those assholes deviated from the plan and decided to take his daughter too. When Benton found out the truth, he was angry at me, angry enough to shoot me. Every time I think the betrayal is behind us, it's resurrected. He hates me all over again—and there's nothing I can do to fix it." He took another drink, his shoulders heavy, his handsome face tight with unease.

"You gave a little girl to drug dealers...?" It really was horrible.

He gave a nod. "The deal was just to keep the mother until Benton and I showed up. Then we would make the trade and both have what we really wanted. But...it didn't go according to plan. It's a long story, but there was another woman there, and she messed everything up. The freaks chose to fake the little girl's death so they could keep both of them—and then everything went to shit."

My heart broke for Benton. I imagined his reaction when he was told that his little girl had been killed.

"In the end, we got Claire and Beatrice back unharmed, and the woman we saved is now his wife. There are times when everything seems fine with Benton, but then the dust gets kicked up and he hates me again." His eyes shifted away, thinking of something else. "He hasn't forgiven me. Never will. Can't say I blame him...but it's shitty."

I processed all that information in silence. It was the first time I realized Bartholomew wasn't that different from my father. He was capable of anything to get what he wanted. "Why would you do that to your friend?"

"Because I felt betrayed. He was my second in an organization that only takes life sentences. He broke his vow and turned his back on me—after everything I did for him." Now his anger showed, burning underneath the surface. "After everything we'd been through, he left me hanging. I never got over it. He left me to be a father to a child he didn't even want. He said I was his brother, but clearly, blood is stronger than whatever the fuck we had…"

If I didn't know so much about him already, his actions would have been ludicrous. But I understood them perfectly. "You're jealous of his daughter."

His eyes narrowed.

"He's the only family you've ever had, but he picked her over you."

He set the empty glass on the table and looked away again.

"It was the only way to get what you wanted. To have Benton back in your life while he remained a father to his daughter. It was the only way for the two of you to share him."

He still wouldn't look at me. "I was promised nothing would happen to Beatrice. And I was also promised it would only be Beatrice, not the little girl. But it's my fault for trusting the word of a psychopath. Doesn't justify the horrible things that little girl saw."

"Why do you keep calling them that? Freaks. Psychopaths."

He considered his answer for a long time. "Because it's a cult. The leaders consider themselves demons, and they capture beautiful women they believe to be angels, the only ones who have the power to restore their redemption with God."

My face must have looked horrified.

"They force the girls to do acid with them. That's how they *ascend*."

Jesus.

"Freaks…that's exactly what they are."

And that little girl had been trapped with them. Horrible. "The fact that you two still talk suggests you're still important to him."

He didn't say anything.

"It makes him angry every time he thinks about it, but after he cools off, he'll come back around."

"He won't accept my apology."

"Maybe he needs more time."

"His brother works for me now—and Benton doesn't like it. I offered to let Bleu go, but Benton doesn't want to interfere in his life... Otherwise, he would be no better than me. Truer words I've never heard."

"Why doesn't he want him to work for you?"

He gave a subtle shrug. "It's not exactly a job that ends in retirement. It's more of a sprint than a marathon."

"But Benton would have stayed if he didn't have his daughter, right?"

"Probably. But I guess fatherhood has given him a new perspective on life."

I saw both light and dark in this man. He was a man willing to do anything to achieve his agenda, but he did have limits, unlike my father.

"This is the part where you ask me to leave." He crossed one ankle on the opposite knee, getting more comfortable in the chair like he wasn't going anywhere. "To walk out of your life and never come back."

I'd known from the very beginning I shouldn't get involved with a man like him, but here I was, six weeks later, needing our nights together more than I needed air or water. Handsome men who passed me suddenly appeared faceless, just a blur because my thoughts were wholly occupied by Bartholomew. "My father would have taken the girl himself and threatened to hurt her if Benton didn't cooperate. And he would have kept that threat over his head every single day to ensure his compliance. He would have been a dictator and Benton a slave. You're better than that."

"Just because I'm not as evil as your father doesn't make me a good guy, sweetheart." His jawline was covered with a shadow that went down his neck. It had the same darkness as his eyes.

"You didn't mean for Claire to be taken."

"What I did was fucked up, nonetheless."

"They told you they wouldn't hurt Beatrice—"

"And I was foolish for believing that."

"How is she now?" I asked.

Bartholomew stared. And stared.

I must have said the wrong thing.

"Gone. She abandoned Claire and moved to London."

"Why?"

"She never wanted to be a mother. She'd wanted an abortion, but Benton asked her to keep it. She was tortured at the camp, and her mind broke once she came home. She was definitely unsuitable for motherhood then."

What a sad story. What a terrible thing for Claire to go through.

"Maybe that outcome was inevitable—but I sure moved things along."

My arms crossed over my chest, thinking about my own mother, how much she loved me, how she never wanted to leave me.

He looked away and let the silence go by.

Despite the horror of his tale, it didn't change my opinion of him. "I don't want you to leave."

His eyes slowly came back to me.

"I hope things work out with Benton."

"If you were the one stuck in that cult, I think you would feel differently."

"Maybe. But I'm here now—and I can see how sorry you are."

"No amount of remorse will be equivalent to the injury I caused. If I were Benton, I would do more than shoot me. He's already shown me mercy I haven't earned."

"Because he loves you."

He wore a cold look.

"Because he knows you just miss him."

"We aren't pussies, so don't talk about us like we are."

"There's nothing wrong with loving your friend and him loving you back."

His visage remained cold, like my descriptions of their relationship were truly annoying him.

I dropped it. "I'm sorry you had a bad night, but make no mistake, if you talk to me like that again, I'll be the one to hang up on you."

He watched me, his intelligent eyes glued to mine.

"And we'll be done."

Now his coldness disappeared, and a glimmer of affection sparkled in his eyes. He preferred my hardness to my softness, seemed to enjoy it when I put him in his place. "Understood."

I didn't realize I'd fallen asleep until I felt him move.

My eyes opened to see Bartholomew sliding from the bed, doing his best to leave without waking me up.

"Where do you think you're going?" I grabbed his chiseled forearm, feeling all the cords of his tight skin. I tugged him back to bed, wanting that heat to warm my sheets again.

He came back to me, the corner of his mouth slightly raised in a smile.

I hugged him to me, the two of us sharing a single pillow, my leg hiked up over his hip. My fingers immediately dug into his thick hair.

"I have to go, sweetheart. But I'll wait for you to fall asleep again."

"Go where?" I asked, missing our time in Florence when he was beside me every night, when I woke up to his body next to mine. He wasn't a vampire, just a man beside his woman.

He stared at me with those dark eyes, thinking an answer wasn't necessary.

"You're the boss. Can't you just not show up?"

"I could, but I already took a hiatus longer than I should have when we went to Florence. There's a lot of shit that needs my attention, and I'm the only one who can get things done."

"I miss sleeping with you." It was like our fight had never happened. I was immediately attached and clingy, something I'd never been before. There was always this distance between us, a constant reminder that this was a clandestine affair that would be snuffed out like a breeze to a lit candle. He was a lover to pass the time, a man who would be replaced by my future husband. He would be a memory, a good time, a story to share with my girlfriends.

"Become a vampire and you can sleep with me all you want."

"I don't think my clients would be too happy about that."

He rolled me onto my back and settled on top of me, his thighs separating mine as he positioned himself to enter me.

"I thought you were leaving..."

He guided himself inside and sank, his big dick entering my soreness. "Don't beg a man to stay unless you're looking to get fucked again."

I arrived at the apartment with the clothes on hangers, protected in a plastic bag. The staff let me inside, and I made my way upstairs to put everything in Hayes's closet. It was a suit for a charity dinner he had, as well as a couple collared shirts for his more casual events.

I helped myself to his closet, hanging everything in the open section inside. When I walked out, he stood in the center of his bedroom, wearing sweatpants low on his hips with a black t-shirt on top.

I'd seen him shirtless a couple times, and it was a delicious sight. But now I didn't feel anything—because Bartholomew was a million times sexier. "Good morning, Hayes. I hung up your things in the closet. You're gonna look great tomorrow night."

"Thanks, Laura." His hair was still messy because he seemed to roll out of bed and head straight to his office to get to work. He was some kind of investment banker who'd opened his own company. He had an office in

Paris as well as the US, so he traveled back and forth a lot. "I was wondering if I could ask you for a favor."

"Of course. How can I help?" I hoped he didn't need another outfit for tomorrow, because I'd have to bust my ass to make that happen in such a short amount of time.

"Would you join me tomorrow?" he asked. "My ex will be there, and I'd rather not go stag."

Weren't there a million girls he could ask? "I'm surprised you don't have anyone else to ask." Not only was he young and rich, but he was handsome. Could get laid by a different girl every night of the week.

"I feel like the other girls I know try too hard...if that makes any sense."

Tried too hard to get a ring on their finger, probably. "Hayes, I'd love to help you out, but I try to keep my professional and personal lives separate."

He gave a nod, but there was a flash of disappointment. "Yes, I understand." He turned to walk away, his shoulders dropped like a wounded animal.

I felt so guilty that I changed my mind. "I'll go with you, but just this one time."

He turned back around, a smile bright on his face. "Thank you, Laura. I appreciate it."

I sat at my vanity in my bedroom and clipped the earrings into place. My hair was in open curls, and I wore a black dress with my favorite necklace. I'd chosen something understated, still trying to look professional in my evening wear. If I were going out with Bartholomew, I would have chosen something very different, something that would drive him crazy until he snapped and took me against the bathroom wall.

Knock. Knock. Knock.

I was supposed to meet at Hayes's place, but maybe he'd forgotten what I said and came to pick me up instead. I got my heels on fast and hooked in the straps before I opened the door to let him in. "Hi—" My voice died in my throat when I saw it wasn't Hayes on the doorstep— but Bartholomew.

His eyes immediately took me in, raking my body from head to toe, taking his time like he wanted me to feel the heat of his gaze. He was in his signature look, black on black, looking like a bad boy with a motorcycle parked out front. "Is this a bad time?"

He'd started to come by unannounced, just dropping by whenever he had some free time during his night. I was usually home working on my laptop, so I didn't mind the unexpected visits, but now I was caught between a rock and a hard place. "I was just about to leave, actually."

"Leave for what?" He welcomed himself into my apartment, his boots like anvils against the hardwood floor with every step he took.

"I have an event tonight. For work."

"I didn't realize that was part of your job description."

"Not usually, but it happens." Agreeing to be Hayes's date for this dinner had felt innocent at the time, but now that I was in the room with Bartholomew, I realized how bad it would look if I told him about my plans. He would lose his shit just the way he did with Victor.

He took a seat in one of the dining chairs and looked at me. "What's the event for?"

"Charity."

"And this involves you how…?"

It was like he knew. I swear, this man knew everything. "One of my clients asked me to go with him. These events are a great way for me to be introduced to other people who need my services. On average, I'll probably get twenty inquiries in a single night, so it's great business for me."

Bartholomew had clearly stopped listening after he'd heard the first sentence. His face was still, but his fair skin started to flush with a faint redness. Like a black hole, he sucked all the light and energy out of the room, ready to eject it as a bomb any second. "*Him?*"

"His name is Hayes—"

"Did I ask for his name?"

"Bartholomew—"

"Why the fuck are you going with him?" He was out of the chair, facing off with me.

"He just got divorced—"

"What does that matter?"

"He asked me to go with him as a favor—"

"He asked you to go with him so he can fuck you."

I rolled my eyes. "That's not why he asked—"

"Trust me." He looked me up and down again. "That's exactly why he asked."

"Even if that were true, just because he wants to fuck me doesn't mean he gets to—"

"But he gets to hold your waist and show you off like you're his—when you're fucking mine."

This was so bad. "You need to calm down—"

"You need to remember who you're dealing with, Laura. I put men in oil drums and dump them out in the ocean. If you don't want that to happen to your little friend, I suggest you call this thing off."

"I already agreed to go with him—"

"Then unagree."

I turned away from him, sick of his rage. "I'm going with him as a friend. It's a great opportunity for me to meet other prospective clients who might need my services, and unlike you, I'm not a billionaire, so I need all the help I can get."

"You want money? I can get you ten million in cash in the next hour."

"Oh my god..." My hands went to my hips. "All I want from you is you—not your money."

He stared at me, his breaths growing so deep they were noticeable.

"You're acting like a psychopath right now."

"Sweetheart, I'm the biggest drug dealer in France. Of course I'm a fucking psychopath."

I walked up to him, seeing him struggle to sheathe his rage. "You don't trust me?" My eyes moved back and forth between his. "You really think I'm looking to replace you with a watered-down banker?"

"That's exactly what you want in a husband, isn't it?" he asked coldly.

I wanted to step back because his comment felt like a slap. "I would think a man like you would be too confident to be jealous—"

"I'm not jealous. I'm possessive. I'm controlling. And I'm selfish. You think I'd let someone else drive my Bugatti? You think I'd give my wealth to those less fortunate? You think I share my power or keep it all for myself? And you expect me to be any different with you? You're mine—and I don't share."

I almost cowered and called the whole thing off. "Look, he's a big client of mine, and I can't abandon him at the last minute—"

"Then I'll be your fucking client."

"I have to keep my word, Bartholomew. This will be the last time, I promise."

He was furious. It was all in his eyes.

"I'm sorry."

He turned around and walked out of my apartment, but he made sure to slam the door before he left.

It was a boring party.

Hayes introduced me to some people, and I was able to make connections with potential clients. He knew a lot of rich people, which was exactly the clientele I was looking for. People who were too busy to pick out their clothes and could easily afford a professional making them look good for all their occasions. Some of them were bankers. Others were business owners. The types of people that had businesses you never heard of but made them millionaires.

I kept thinking about Bartholomew. I feared our next conversation. I feared there wouldn't be another conversation…

We had dinner and drinks, and at some point, Hayes pointed out his ex-wife.

She was a pretty blonde, and it looked like she had already moved on to husband #2.

The second Hayes saw that, he started to drink more… and more. The only person I saw drink like that was Bartholomew, but I suspected Hayes couldn't hold his liquor the way he could. We eventually cut the night short, and the driver took us back to his place.

I hoped he would drop me off on the way, but he was probably too depressed to think about anyone else but himself.

Whatever, I'd take a cab.

His driver pulled in past the gates to his estate, and then he headed inside. An elevator took us to the ground floor, so I stepped out and prepared to walk out to the street and order a ride.

"Well, thanks for coming," he said, hands in his pockets.

"Of course. I was able to connect with a lot of potential clients, so that's great for business."

He gave a nod.

"I'm sorry about your ex."

"Took half my money…and then half my heart."

I didn't know what to say to that. "Things will get better, Hayes."

"Yeah? I'd like to believe that, but…"

I stood there awkwardly, unsure what to do. The extent of my relationship with Hayes was small talk and measurements. I wouldn't really consider us to be friends. "Well, good night."

"It's late…if you want to stay."

Uh, awkward. "I've already ordered a ride. They'll be here any minute."

He gave a nod. "Well, I really appreciate your coming with me."

"I'm happy to help—"

He grabbed me by the arm and leaned in.

I dodged out of the way so quick that he almost toppled over.

Fuck, Bartholomew was right. "Uh, I should go. Good night, Hayes." I headed for the entryway before he could say anything more. I kept my word because I didn't want to lose Hayes as a client, but now I'd lost him anyway… and put my relationship in jeopardy.

He didn't take my calls.

I called him once a day, at the beginning of the evening when I knew he started his day. It went to voice mail every time. I never called him more than once because I didn't want to blow up his phone and show my desperation.

But I was definitely desperate.

Please talk to me. I fired off the text message, even though I knew there would be no reply.

And there wasn't.

It'd been three days, and now I worried that our relationship was over. He'd disappeared from my life as quickly as he'd come into it. The most passionate relationship of my life had been ruined by my compassion.

Had been ruined for nothing.

Even though I knew the relationship would never be more than a dirty secret, it still hurt to watch it fall apart. He was never going to be my husband or the father of my children. He was always going to be a memory that I would think about from time to time.

But it still sucked.

I miss you.

Every time my phone rang, I hoped it was Bartholomew. It always gave me a jump, a small jolt of excitement. But now five days had come and gone, and I hadn't heard from him. I stood at the counter in my office and looked at the screen of my lit phone, seeing a number I didn't recognize.

I always took every call, because it could be a potential client trying to connect with me, so I answered. "This is Laura."

"Hey, Laura." I recognized that voice. Could never forget it. "It's Victor."

"Yeah, I recognized your voice. What's up?" I moved to my chair behind my desk.

"I'm not sure what happened, but Catherine got beat up pretty badly."

My heart somersaulted into my stomach. "What...?"

"We've got a lot of shit on our plate right now, and with Lucas still hurt, work has been difficult. I'm not sure if it's the stress of that...or maybe your sister provoked him... I don't know."

"*Provoked him?*" Was there any justification for barbarism?

"I just thought you should know."

My ex-husband called me, and my own father didn't. Or did he even care? "How is she?"

"She's got a broken arm and a bruised face. She's home from the hospital and resting."

"And my father's response?" I asked, hearing my voice rise because I already knew the answer.

"Like I said...there's a lot of shit going down right now."

There was always a lot of shit going down. "Worthless piece of shit. I'm coming down."

"To do what?"

"I'm not sure. To kill Lucas. To get my sister out of there. To push my father out a window. Maybe all of the above."

I packed a small bag and headed for the airport. There were several flights to Florence on a daily basis, so I was able to get a last-minute flight and head to the capital of the Renaissance. For a brief second, I assumed I would stay at Bartholomew's apartment, but then I remembered we weren't a thing anymore.

I'd forgotten about it in the heat of my anger.

Now the painful feelings returned in a tidal wave, drowning me with regret and sorrow. Bartholomew didn't beat me to death with his fists or stuff me in an oil drum, but he still crushed me with his cruel punishment. He dropped me without further conversation, ghosted me like I'd never meant anything to him.

God, it hurt.

When I landed in Florence, I grabbed my suitcase from baggage claim and headed outside to grab a taxi. The automatic doors opened, the warm air hit me in the face, and then I walked to the curb as I pulled my luggage with me.

I halted in my tracks when I saw him.

In a black t-shirt and jeans, his signature boots on his feet. He stuck out in the sea of regular people, deadly handsome, tall like a cypress tree from ancient times. His eyes were like bullets—and my face was the target.

I stopped breathing altogether. My body forgot how to function. I was shocked to see him—and a little scared.

I had so many questions, but I didn't dare ask a single one.

He opened the back door to the SUV at the curb. "Get in."

The drive was spent in silence.

He kept his gaze out his window. Left the space between us. Acted as if I weren't there. The driver didn't ask him any questions. His knees were wide apart, and his elbow rested on the armrest. His fingertips were curled around his mouth. Sunglasses sat on the bridge of his nose, so his eyes were impossible to decipher.

I was so nervous I felt like I'd been kidnapped.

We passed through his gate onto his property, and then one of the guys took my bags. The two of us entered his home, and his butler didn't come to greet us, which made me think Bartholomew had already been staying here.

He took the stairs first, and when he made it to the next landing and realized I wasn't behind him, he gave me a cold stare.

I didn't need to be asked twice.

We entered his bedroom, the place where I'd slept beside him for the first time, the terrace doors open like he'd been sitting there before he'd left to pick me up at the airport. It smelled the way it did before, with a hint of his cologne, the scent of clean sheets and fresh flowers.

He turned around and faced me.

Looked at me like he hated me.

I'd never been the type to cower, but that look on his face made me suddenly shy.

"What are you doing here?"

Both of my eyebrows rose, because that was a question I should ask instead of being asked. "To see my sister. What are *you* doing here?"

He never answered the question—no surprise there.

"Why did you bring me here?"

Silence.

"You haven't taken my calls. Responded to my texts…" I tried to disguise the hurt in my voice with anger, but I wasn't angry at all, just sad.

"Because I didn't want to. I still don't want to, but you forced my hand."

"You didn't have to pick me up from the airport. You didn't have to bring my stuff here. You didn't have to do anything—"

"I'm going to talk now—and you're going to listen."

If I didn't miss him so much, I'd push back. But we stood on fragile ground, and if there was any chance I could get him back, I didn't want to screw it up.

"Loyalty. I demand it from my men. I demand it from my allies. And I demand it from my lovers. If you can't give that to me, then we're done."

"I am loyal to you—"

"I talk. You listen." He took a step toward me, his hard face slightly red in anger. "Was I unclear?"

I wasn't sure if it was a trick question. I chose to stay quiet—and that seemed to be the right answer.

His eyes flicked back and forth between mine before he continued. "If you want to be my woman, then you follow my rules and meet my expectations. If a woman asked me to be her date as a *favor*, you bet your ass the answer would be no. While you sleep at night, I get offers left and right, and I tell them to piss off. You think I let them down easily? You think I protect their egos? No. I say I have a woman. Simple as that."

"I—"

His eyes flashed.

Shit.

He stared me down to make sure that my mouth was closed. "You get *one* pass. That's it. The only language I understand is loyalty. Show me loyalty—or I walk away. Understood?"

"Can I explain myself—"

"No. Now answer my question."

"Is this how you talk to your other lovers?"

His eyes flicked back and forth between mine. "I don't know. There's never been anyone else."

My eyes mirrored his. "Then...who were they?"

"Whores. One-night stands. Women whose names I don't remember."

So this was just as new for him as it was for me. "Can I say something—"

"The conversation is over, Laura."

"Goddammit, let me talk!"

Despite my loud outburst, he remained still. Only his eyes moved.

"I'm sorry. I just wanted you to know that..."

His eyes finally dropped their hostility. He was still guarded, but he wasn't an angry bull anymore.

"You were right. It was disrespectful to you. I wouldn't like it if some woman asked you to be her date to get back at her ex...or just wanted your company...or whatever the reason may be."

Now he didn't interrupt me.

"At the end of the night, he tried to kiss me. I felt so stupid."

Instead of exploding in a blind rage, his expression hadn't changed.

"I think he was just drunk and depressed and didn't mean it...but still."

He remained quiet.

"I doubt he even remembered it the next day."

"Is he still your client?"

"I haven't let him go yet. If he contacts me, I'll tell him. But I'm hoping he's too embarrassed to say anything."

He was closed off and quiet, regarding me from the distance he'd put between us.

"I really missed you..." The hurt escaped my voice this time because there was no anger to mask it. "When you ghosted me...I was devastated." I felt like I'd lost a piece of myself. Something substantial. Like my heart or my soul.

"I wish I could say the same—but I was too angry."

"Are you…still angry?" There were only a few steps between us, but it felt like miles. A yearning burned in my chest, a need I'd never felt before in my life. I could have counted my blessings that this drug lord was finally out of my life—but I didn't feel that way in the least.

After a stretch of silence, he moved toward me, his heat and scent coming closer, close enough for me to feel and smell. When his hand cupped my face and directed my lips toward him, I felt my legs turn to jelly. The gnawing started in my stomach, the tightness that formed before my body released in a swell of pleasure.

He kissed me.

It started off slow, an introduction between our mouths, but that didn't last long. Soon, his fingers were deep in my hair and his kiss turned ravenous. His arm secured itself around my back, and he pulled me flush against his body, wanting me to feel how *unangry* he was.

All the wanting and all the waiting…was finally over.

As he guided me backward to the bed, pieces of clothing left his body. His shirt disappeared, and my hands got to explore his chest. His boots were kicked aside, and then his jeans were torn off. Soon, I had his throbbing dick in my hand, and my thumb caught a drop that oozed from the tip.

He stripped me naked before he got me on the bed, my back to the mattress, my legs around his waist. This seemed to be his favorite position because he was always the one to initiate it. He directed his thick length inside me and was immediately met with a rush of viscous desire. It smoothed his entry, making him close his eyes briefly as he enjoyed it. "Sweetheart…" He sank until he was fully sheathed, reclaiming my body as his.

My fingers dug into his hair and I kissed him. "Babe, I'm sorry…"

He rocked his hips and started to move inside me, deep and even strokes, taking his time rather than fucking me hard into the mattress. He breathed against my mouth as he moved. "I know."

20

LAURA

I'd momentarily forgotten the reason I came here in the first place.

He was on top. Then I was on top. We switched back and forth, and our rendezvous ended with my ass in the air at the edge of the bed. Back-to-back, with little conversation in between, we caught up on all the time we'd missed.

It was the first time I'd breathed easy in a week.

How could being with such a dangerous man make me feel complete?

We ended up in the shower, luxurious and spacious with its two showerheads. He rubbed the bar of soap over his chiseled body, making the soap bubble and lather until it streaked down his beautiful body. He was so tight, his muscles, his skin, the cords of his veins.

Talk about tall, dark, and handsome...

His eyes caught mine, watching me stare at him. "Is your sister okay?"

My predicament came tumbling back. "No. Apparently, Lucas broke her arm and bloodied her face pretty badly." Maybe I would take one of Bartholomew's guns and shoot Lucas in the stomach the second I saw him. "I gotta get her outta here. Or I gotta kill Lucas. Maybe both."

"Your father did nothing?"

"Nope. Apparently, he's too focused on some crisis he's having."

"He cared enough to call you."

"He wasn't the one who called," I blurted without thinking.

Bartholomew was sure to draw the correct conclusion, but he didn't react. He seemed more concerned about the wellbeing of my sister. "I'll take care of it for you."

"How?"

"However you want." His dark eyes looked at me with utter calm, like he'd offered to pick me up a couple apples while he was at the market. "I can kill him. I can torture him. I can torture him and then kill him… Whatever you want."

As tempting as that was, it wasn't that simple. "It was one thing when you hurt Lucas, but if you kill him, my father will hunt you down with everything he has."

A glimmer of a smile moved on to his lips. "Fine with me."

"You would make your life complicated just for me?"

"Complicated is all I know," he said. "I'm not sure how useful Lucas really is to your father anyway. The guys who hit their women are always cowards. Not exactly useful in the thick of things."

"Well, my father thinks he's useful."

"Then your father has poor judgment. But you already knew that." He finished with the shower then stepped out. He grabbed the towel and quickly rubbed down his body, catching the drops on his chest and legs before ruffling his hair with the cotton.

It was hard not to stare. I turned off the water and joined him. "I'm afraid my sister will never forgive me if I get him killed."

"She doesn't have to know it's you. Or me, to be exact."

"After I told everyone you hurt Lucas for me, they'll figure it out."

He secured the towel around his waist then looked at his appearance in the mirror, totally oblivious to how damn sexy he was. It was just another day for him. Another shave. "Then I can give him a warning." He smeared the cream all over his face then began to shave, using a basic razor instead of an electric one. He was a rich man but one with simple taste. "A verbal warning."

"And you think that'll work?"

His eyes met mine in the mirror before he continued to shave his jawline.

Guess so. "You never told me why you're in the city."

He continued to shave, ignoring what I'd said.

I stared at his reflection in the mirror, pressing him to give me an answer.

He seemed to feel my gaze because he said, "Business."

"I thought France was your territory." He was the biggest distributor in France, and I knew who the biggest distributor was in Italy. My father had been the Skull King since I could remember. Being his daughter exposed me to things I shouldn't have seen. Exposed me to information I shouldn't have had—especially when I was only eleven years old.

He washed his face, applied his aftershave, and then patted his skin dry with a towel. Now his chiseled jawline was on full display, the hard bones in his face distinguished through the tight skin. The cords in his neck were more pronounced too. He tossed the towel on the counter then turned to face me so our eyes could meet.

"Are you going to answer my question?"

He walked past me out of the bathroom, dropping his towel along the way. "No."

"What the fuck is wrong with you?" I yelled at my father in his own home, screaming in the drawing room. "He broke Catherine's arm. He beat her face until it turned black and blue. And yet, you continue to employ this asshole? Why isn't he buried six feet under? As a girl dad, aren't you supposed to be overprotective and all those other clichés?"

He had a bored look on his face, like he hadn't listened to a word I said. "It's not important right now."

"Not important...?" I couldn't believe the words out of his mouth. "He could *kill* her."

He turned to face me, his face subtly enraged. "I don't have time for this conversation, but I made time—out of respect for you."

"Oh wow... I feel so loved."

"This nonsense with Lucas and Catherine can wait until another time—"

"*Nonsense?* It's domestic abuse. I gotta ask, did you hit Mom? Because you seem real chill about the whole thing."

My father blinked. That was it. Nothing else.

"Oh my god...you did."

"No, Laura." He lost his temper. "I refuse to even respond to an accusation so ridiculous—"

"Protect your daughter. Be a man, goddammit."

He rushed me, like he was going to bloody me the way Lucas did to his other daughter. But he stopped. Went still. The fight ensued beneath his features.

I stood my ground and dared him to fuck with me. "Do it. See what happens." Bartholomew would walk right into this house and carve every feature off his face if he laid a hand on me.

His eyes flicked back and forth between mine. "Don't insult me like that again."

"You want my respect? Then earn it."

His face scrunched together in rage, like there was too much to contain, too much to express. "I've lost my relationship with my production partners because some asshole has undermined me. No one will do business with me, not the US, not even Russia. I have no product to put on the streets, so the livelihood of everyone who works for me is in jeopardy. My own livelihood is in jeopardy. No cash is coming in, but cash is pouring out, funding this very expensive enterprise. If I don't find a solution soon, I'll have to start selling my homes one by one, because if I lose my men and my protection, I'll be dead. So, I don't give a fuck about your sister right now. If she doesn't like the way Lucas treats her, she can leave. Simple as that."

I breathed as I processed all of that, realizing it was a real situation, nothing like the ones I remembered from my childhood. I didn't know what to say—because something about it didn't sit right with me.

A hand grabbed me by the arm. "Let's go, Laura."

I let Victor pull me, my mind still in a haze.

He escorted me to the entryway. "It's really not the best time, Laura."

"Do you know who's behind this?"

"No one's naming names. And they can't be bought—because the other guy is always outbidding us for secrecy."

My father had a lot of enemies, but none that had this kind of power. "I want to see Catherine. Can you take me to her? I don't know where she lives, and I don't have her number either."

He nodded. "Let's make it quick because I'm needed elsewhere."

He dropped me off at her apartment.

It was a nice piece of real estate, something that rivaled Bartholomew's place. It was soaked in wealth, and now it made perfect sense why my sister was under my father's thumb. She couldn't live without this kind of luxury.

I missed it sometimes, but it wasn't worth the price.

I asked the butler to see her, but when he returned, he denied my request. "Catherine is resting right now. Perhaps another time."

She was blowing me off—and for good reason. "I don't think so." I walked around him and marched in the direction I'd seen him disappear.

"Stop! She wants you to leave."

I ignored him and kept going, finding her in a sitting room, wearing her athleisure as she sat on the couch, her arm in a cast—and her face black and blue.

The butler made the mistake of grabbing me by the arm.

I twisted out of his grasp like a pro then shoved him in the chest.

He stumbled backward, his eyes wide and affronted. "I'll call security."

"It's fine." Her quiet voice came from the couch. "It's not going to stop her."

"Damn right, it's not." I grabbed one of the armchairs and dragged it close to where she sat. I'd been so focused on getting here that I didn't anticipate how I would feel once I arrived—once I saw how terrible she looked.

For the first time in my life, I was at a loss for words.

Catherine couldn't look at me. She avoided eye contact as the silence deepened.

"Catherine..." I expected grand words to leave my mouth, but they never did.

"It's not as bad as it looks."

"Really?" The comment snapped me out of my astonishment. "Because your arm is in a cast since it's broken. And the reason your face is all those different colors is because it's bleeding and healing at the same time. Yes, it's as bad as it looks."

She wasn't going to look at me now.

"Why do you put up with this?"

"Because I love him."

Jesus. "Well, in case you haven't figured this out, he doesn't love you."

"He just gets angry—"

"I'm angry right now, but am I hitting you?"

She just sat there.

"Catherine, look at me—"

"I don't need your judgments right now."

"I'm not judging you for being in this situation. You think you're the first woman who's stuck with a man who wasn't taught how to control his emotions? Who wasn't taught how to be a man? You aren't. But I do judge you for not loving yourself enough to realize you deserve more. You deserve a man who defends you from assholes like this." Like my man...who'd killed the men who ruined my life.

"I'm already married—"

"Half of marriages end in divorce."

"Well, you know we don't believe in divorce—"

"Not *we*. Don't include me in that. I believe a woman should be free of violence and disrespect, and if that means getting a divorce, so be it. Don't allow Father's religious bullshit to trap you. He says he's a man of faith, but he's putting drugs on the street and killing anyone who opposes him. He's a goddamn hypocrite—so there's no reason you can't be free."

"It's complicated…"

"Complicated how?"

"If I divorce Lucas, Father will be so ashamed of me he'll take all of this away." She gestured to the home she occupied, the multimillion-euro palace that people envied. "What will I do then?"

"Get a job. Support yourself. Just like everyone else, Catherine." I tried to keep the sarcasm out of my voice. Judging her wouldn't improve her situation.

"I don't want to be poor."

"I'm poor, and I'm perfectly fine. I have a little apartment in Paris, live paycheck to paycheck, and it's okay. It's not as bad as you think."

"Then you've forgotten what it's like to be rich."

"And you have no idea how liberating it is to be your own person, to have the independence that makes you free of other people's subjugation. Father has no power over me because I don't need his money. You know how satisfying that is?"

She adjusted her cast, picking at a piece of thread that had come loose.

"And you don't have to be poor, Catherine. Start a business. Hustle. Grow your wealth. You're so young that you can start over and chase your dreams. You love fashion—and you're so close to the capital of the fashion world."

"Easier said than done."

"Catherine, think about it like this." I waited for her to look at me before I continued. "If you don't do something different, then nothing will be different. Everything is guaranteed to stay the same. This cast will be replaced by a new one. Future bruises will replace the ones you wear now. And one day...he might kill you.

That's your future, Catherine. That's it. Nothing more. Nothing less. But if you leave and start over, it will be different. It might be better. It might be worse. But at least it'll be different. You can always come and live with me in Paris—"

"What the fuck are you doing in my house?" Lucas appeared, shirtless and in just his sweatpants, a gauze still wrapped around his torso from where Bartholomew had stabbed him. He was bulky, muscle on muscle.

But I wasn't the least bit scared.

"Get away from my wife."

Catherine immediately cowered, looking away from me as if dismissing me, trying to be as small as possible so she could disappear.

Not me. I got big. And I got loud. I rose to my feet and faced off with him.

"What are you saying to my wife?" He came closer, his muscular arms at his sides, the skin tinting red with adrenaline. "What ridiculous ideas are you putting in her head—"

"That she deserves better than the coward she married."

His eyes seared like a hot frying pan. He came closer to me. "Coward, huh?"

"You're going to prove you aren't by beating another woman? Really impressive."

"You better watch your fucking mouth—"

"Or what?" I moved toward him.

Catherine's scared voice came from the couch. "Laura..."

"Or what?" he asked. "How about I break that mouth of yours so I don't have to listen to it anymore—"

I slapped him hard across the face.

He turned with the hit then backed up in shock. His furious eyes returned to me, in disbelief that I had the audacity to hit him. Then he came toward me, ready to make good on his word.

"Lay a hand on me, and see what happens."

He stopped dead in his tracks.

"Do it. Make me black and blue. Break my jaw. Let me go home to my man and show him what you've done to me."

Powerless to do anything other than stare at me with a pissed-off look on his face, he just stood there, invisible ropes tying his hands back.

"That's what I thought." I walked right up to him—and spat on his face.

He flinched like he wanted to hit me, but he wiped the saliva from his face instead.

"I'm coming for you, Lucas." I walked past him as I made my exit. "Or should I say...my man is coming for you."

21

BARTHOLOMEW

"Everything is set." Bleu sat in the armchair closest to the cold fireplace.

My men filled the room, some sitting on the windowsills, others occupying the couches, some standing in the corners. The armchair was mine—and they all knew not to sit there. I looked at Bleu's blue eyes, identical to his brother's, but they were different in every other way.

He couldn't replace what I'd lost.

The door to the study opened, and instead of seeing my butler enter to make an announcement, it was Laura.

She stilled when she realized what she'd just walked into.

Armed men in every corner. A tense silence that punctured her skin the second she felt the atmosphere. They were all pivoted to face me, my presence the sun in this galaxy. Her eyes quickly flicked to all the men standing there before she looked at me. Without saying a word, she closed the door and retreated.

"Excuse me." I finished my drink then left the room, leaving the men to occupy themselves in my absence. She was already up the stairs and gone by the time I made it into the hallway, so I headed to my bedroom, where she would be waiting for me.

When I entered, she was sitting on the couch, her heels already on the floor beside her.

"I hope I didn't interrupt anything," she said without looking at me, like she was afraid of me.

She'd grown up with strange men positioned all over her childhood home, so this shouldn't be any different. But it disturbed her because she'd never witnessed me in my element before. All she knew about me was what I shared with her, but she'd never seen me in action. She'd never watched me command a room. Never watched me break a skull under my boot. Never watched me raise my voice when my men failed to execute my wishes. It was a solemn reminder of the man she was fucking.

"Did you see your sister?"

"Yes." Her eyes were still elsewhere, even though I sat directly across from her.

That was all she gave me. Nothing else. That was when I knew something was wrong. "Sweetheart?"

After a breath, she turned her head to regard me. With a steely gaze, she stared at me, her eyes shielded as if behind protective glass. "I'm going to ask you something—and you're going to tell me the truth."

"You don't need to command my honesty, not when I've never lied to you."

Her eyes dropped, thinking everything over in her head.

I could read the unease in her beautiful face, saw the way she tried to process the horrible truth. She hadn't asked the question because she wasn't ready for the answer yet. She was a smart woman and had connected the dots on her own, but it wouldn't be real until I confirmed her terrible suspicions. "Yes."

Her eyes lifted again.

"It's me."

Her eyes were still before she swallowed. Her gaze remained steady, but only for a short while. Then she lost her bearings quickly, looking at anything else but me. Her hand rubbed her arm, her knees came close together, and she continued to struggle with the affirmation she'd asked for. "This whole time..." She shook her head, like her disagreement would make it untrue. "You knew exactly who I was when you walked into my shop..."

"Yes."

Now her eyes were glued to the floor, and she looked like she might cry. "Jesus..."

"Laura—"

She got to her feet and prepared to walk out barefoot.

"Laura."

She ignored me and headed to the door.

"Let me explain."

"Fuck off."

I went after her, grabbing her by the arm when she was in the hallway.

She spun out of my grasp and shoved me. Threw her arms against stone. Tried to pry herself free from my strong body, the tears starting to spring from her eyes.

"You're free to go after we talk. Not before."

"Don't tell me what to do—"

"I can do whatever I damn well please. Now sit your ass on the couch." I guided her back into the bedroom with my hand on her arm. I shut the door behind us, and this time, I blocked it so she couldn't run back into the hallway.

She looked at the door behind me, trying to plan her escape. "You give me your word?"

"Yes."

She finally turned away from the door and dropped onto the couch.

This conversation had been approaching on the horizon, the colors growing brighter the closer they came. I'd been ready for it, and I'd been ready for her to piece together the puzzle on her own. My woman wasn't just a smokeshow—she was smart too.

I grabbed a decanter of scotch and two glasses and set them on the coffee table between us.

She didn't look at me as I filled both glasses.

"When I walked into that shop, I had an agenda. To use you to get what I wanted from your father."

Her eyes flicked back to me.

"I abandoned that plan the second I had you. Everything between us—it's been real. Not once have I asked you for information about your father. Not once have I used you to further my plans. Our relationship has been completely separate from my ambitions."

"And you just assumed I would be okay with you trying to ruin my father and take his business?"

"You've made it very clear you don't like him. I didn't think it was an issue."

"*Didn't think it was an issue...*" She gave a slight nod, repeating the words I just spoke. "Right..."

"Separation of church and state."

"Again, you just assumed I would be okay with this. That's ludicrous."

"You've made it very clear that this relationship will be short-lived. We're just living in the moment, knowing at some point, we'll go our separate ways with our separate lives. Therefore, I didn't think we needed to discuss this."

"So, when I told you I was raped—"

"Yes, I already knew."

"You already knew everything about me...and just pretended you didn't?" she asked in disbelief. "And then you insist that we were real?"

"Because we were. We still are. I walked into your office to figure out what I could get out of you, but the second you got on your knees to measure my inseam, that was the furthest thing from my mind. All I wanted to do was fuck you. And then after I fucked you, I wanted to fuck you again...and again."

She looked away.

"I want to fuck you right now." If she walked out of my life forever once this conversation was over, I wasn't sure how I would recover. We hadn't spoken for those five days, and in that time, I'd behaved like a complete lunatic. She was the sedative I needed to tranquilize my rage, and she was the stimulant that made my heart race.

"When were you going to tell me?"

"I wasn't. You're my personal life—and this conquest is business. You left this life because you wanted nothing to do with it, so I honestly believed none of it would matter to you. Your uncle's death was shitty timing. If you'd never returned to Florence, you probably wouldn't have figured out what happened for a very long time—and you would never know I had anything to do with it."

"Again…how could you be with me and do this behind my back?"

My answer was cruel, but it was honest. "Because I don't owe you anything. You're a woman I'm sleeping with—that's it."

Her eyes flashed like my words carved into her skin.

"And you don't owe me anything either."

"So, if I told my father all of this while pretending to play dumb with you, you wouldn't take it personally?" she asked, eyebrow raised. "Because it's just business?"

"Yes."

Her eyes flashed again.

"If you tell him everything the second you leave this apartment, I wouldn't take that personally either. Nor would I care—because I already have his balls in my hand. His fate is sealed in a stone tomb at this point."

She continued to breathe hard, overwhelmed by everything that had just happened. "Why are you doing this?"

"I've expanded my business to Croatia. I want to do the same here."

"And those two places aren't enough for you?" she asked incredulously.

She had rich clients who made their millions and billions running skyscrapers and stashing their wealth in offshore accounts. They were ambitious in their suits and ties and grand boardrooms. But none were nearly as ambitious as me. "Nothing will ever be enough, Laura."

Her hard stare slowly softened, slowly sank into a form of pity.

"I don't intend to kill your father. Just make him work for me."

"That will never happen."

"He'll have no other choice."

"There's always another choice." Her eyes searched mine.

"If he prefers death to subjugation, then that's his business."

"You would let my father die?" She looked strained with her anger.

"You haven't spoken to him in seven years—"

"He's still my father—"

"And he doesn't give a shit about you."

She stilled at the insult, breathed as the pain dug into her skin.

"He doesn't give a shit about your sister. He didn't give a shit about your mom. Power is the only thing that matters to him."

"Just like you." She grabbed the glass and took a drink, her eyes off me.

"I care more about power than he does. But I also care about you more than he does."

Her face turned back to mine.

"You know I'd do anything for you."

"Except abandon this..." Her eyes searched my face, silently pleading with me to drop this agenda and go back to France.

But I couldn't. "No."

"So, you wouldn't do anything for me. Just empty words."

"My professional life is separate from our personal relationship—"

"Just because you're rich doesn't make you a professional. You're a drug dealer who earns his living from the blood and suffering of others."

I had a powerful defense against her claims, but now wasn't the time. "Laura, he doesn't deserve your loyalty. He would sacrifice you in a heartbeat if it moved his pawn across the board. I'm telling you everything you already know."

Her arms crossed over her chest, and she looked down, like she couldn't think when my eyes were on her.

I already knew how this would end. Saw it written all over her face. "You're making a mistake."

Her eyes stayed down. "I-I can't be with someone trying to destroy my family."

"You haven't spoken to him in seven years for a reason—"

"It's not just him, Bartholomew. It's my sister. It's Victor. It's my other family members."

The second she said that asshole's name, I wanted to smash the bottle on the table, but I suppressed the beast that reared its ugly head.

"If you do this...they'll lose everything. I can't live with that. I can't sleep with the man who's intent on destroying my family's power and wealth. My father and I have never seen eye to eye, but this is a different level of betrayal."

"It's not a betrayal because you have nothing to do with it."

"But I'm fucking the man who wants to destroy my family's legacy."

"You ran to Paris because you wanted nothing to do with this life. Now you're defending it? Sounds a bit hypocritical."

The sadness in her eyes was slowly replaced by something else. "If you can't understand the situation you've put me in, then you aren't the man I thought you were. You're narrow-minded and self-absorbed."

She was right on the money.

She looked away again. "This is over." She couldn't look at me and say it. Couldn't watch her sword pierce my flesh.

I'd known it was over the second this conversation started. I'd seen the end at the beginning, but it still hadn't prepared me for the bite of her words. My fingertips felt numb. My body felt empty, all my emotions defeated in a cruel battle. For a relationship that meant nothing, her goodbye hurt like the bullet Benton gave me. "I understand."

She didn't look at me, like she might cry if she did.

"Do what you have to do, sweetheart."

She started to breathe harder, her chest heaving but her eyes dry.

"Just know that I actually give a damn about you—and he never has."

22

LAURA

Bartholomew's driver took me to my father's estate, and I spent the entire drive stifling my silent tears. Some of them escaped my eyes and made rivers down my cheeks. They hit the corners of my lips and made it to my tongue —tasting like salt pellets.

I'd known it was going to end, but when I didn't know when or how, it was easy to forget the impending doom. When I'd woken up that morning with him beside me, I kissed his shoulder to coax him awake, wanting him the second I saw his naked body beside me. But those kisses would be our last.

If I'd known they'd be our last...I wouldn't have left the bed.

The car stopped outside the gate, and I stayed in the back seat as I cleaned up my tears with a tissue. My eyes would be red and my cheeks blotchy, but there was nothing I could do to hide that.

The driver grabbed my bags from the trunk then left me on the sidewalk.

Then he left.

It was really over now.

The guys let me in the gate, pulling my suitcase behind me, walking right into the snake's den. I felt like shit for betraying Bartholomew, but I felt even worse harboring this secret from my own flesh and blood.

Now I wished I'd never met Bartholomew. I wouldn't be in this position. I would be in Paris, thriving in ignorant bliss.

I entered the house, and the butler immediately took my suitcase. "Will you be staying with us, Miss Laura?"

"I hope so." I didn't have anywhere else to go and not a lot of money to spend. "I need to speak to my father."

"He's not in residence right now."

"Then I guess I'll wait."

A couple hours later, he returned. I knew he was home because he was yelling the second he walked through the front door. "To forget everything I've done for him, the years of good business, even the years of bad business... A butter knife will be in his eye before this is over."

Yep, that was my father.

I looked over the balcony of the stairs and saw him storm inside with Victor and some of the other guys.

The butler walked up to him. "Sir—"

"I don't need anything. Get out of my face."

Jackass. "He's trying to tell you that I want to speak with you."

All the men stopped and looked up to where I stood on the stairs.

"And I'm staying in my old room...if that's okay."

My father didn't look excited by my stay. Didn't look upset by it either. His head was somewhere else, deep in the war he was now fighting. He walked on, heading to the drawing room, where the men would smoke cigars and talk shit. Victor lingered, giving me a perplexed expression, but he eventually followed.

I joined them in the drawing room. "I need to speak with Leonardo—alone."

"Laura, now is not the time—"

"I know who's behind this attack."

He let the cigar burn between his fingers as he stared at me, the smoke silently rising toward the ceiling. The other guys sat in silence, spread out across the other couches. Without looking at his men, he raised his hand and silently excused them.

Victor locked eyes with me before he left the room.

My father took a long puff of his cigar before he set it in the ashtray. A cloud of smoke left his lips and rose into the air, infecting the fabric of the furniture and the rugs. "Who?"

I took a seat, the one Victor had just vacated. When I looked at my father, I didn't know how to start, how to be the recipient of that hard gaze. It felt wrong to tell him this, to betray Bartholomew, but then I remembered he was the one who had betrayed me first. He knew everything about me the moment we met—and he'd never intended to tell me. "My boyfriend...Bartholomew." Or my ex-boyfriend, I should say.

His eyes narrowed further, and he said nothing.

I waited for the line of questioning, but it never came.

"I should have known."

"Do you know him?"

"I know of him. Cruel. Ambitious. Maniacal. But I didn't think he would step into our territory."

He did more than step into it from what I'd heard.

"Why are you telling me this?"

"Because..." I'd been played like a fool. "Once I figured out what he was doing, I had to tell you."

"You didn't know?"

I shook my head.

"He used you, Laura. What did you tell him?"

"He's never asked me anything. I think he intended to use me in the beginning, but then our relationship changed."

"Men like that don't change, Laura."

Well, he changed for me. Or at least, it seemed. "I confronted him about my suspicions, and he told me the truth. Once I knew…I couldn't be with a man intent on destroying my family. I know we have our differences… big differences, but I couldn't look the other way on this."

"Because you're loyal." His hand moved to my arm on the couch. It was a touch he hadn't shared with me since I was a little girl. His fingertips were callused from gripping the metal of guns, but they were warm with affection. "It's in your blood." He left his hand there for a while before he withdrew. "Tell me everything about him."

"I honestly don't know anything. He's never shared the details of his professional life with me, and I never asked. But I have witnessed his power and his command. I know he's the kind of man you'd be stupid to fuck with."

"He's sabotaged my relationship with my producers. Paid off everyone else who could help me. He's isolated me, and I know he'll make his move shortly. You're the only leverage I have against him."

"Leverage?" I asked.

"The only thing that might make him reconsider."

"And how would you do that?"

His intelligent eyes bored straight into mine, but he seemed to be thinking about something else, his mind in the distance. An unnecessary silence stretched. That was how deep his thoughts sank. "Ask nicely."

A knock sounded on my bedroom door.

"Come in." I sat on the pillows in the window seat, looking at the lights of the city in the darkness. My bedroom happened to face the direction of Bartholomew's home. I could tell by the placement of the Duomo. I wondered if he sat in his study that very moment, drinking and smoking, wondering if I was thinking about him at the same time.

Yes, I was.

The butler stepped into my bedroom. "Victor is here to see you. Shall I let him in?"

I was in leggings and a baggy sweater, my makeup wiped off my face. But I was too sad to care about my appearance right now. The tears would just ruin my makeup anyway. "That's fine."

Victor entered my bedroom a moment later, dressed in a black t-shirt and dark jeans. He slowly approached the window seat, his hands in his pockets. His eyes roamed over me like they had before, trying to determine my state of mind.

"I'm fine." Even I knew I was lying, so he did too.

He grabbed the armchair and pulled it toward the window so we could sit together. My bedroom was now a guest bedroom, but it was still as immaculate as a primary suite. His elbows rested on the armrests, and he looked out the window before looking at me, back and forth, trying to decide what to say. "I'm sorry this has happened to you."

"It is what it is."

"I was a shitty husband, and then this guy used you."

That wasn't how I would describe it. "We just have conflicting goals in life. We knew it wasn't going to last forever. So I'm not surprised it's over, just surprised how it became over."

"He still deceived you."

"He kept our relationship separate from his ambitions. He did it as long as he could, because once I figured out the truth, he knew it would be over. If he really was an asshole, he could have kept me against my will. But he let me go...knowing I would tell my father everything."

"You keep defending him."

"Just explaining."

"Why did you end the relationship if he did nothing wrong?"

"Because..." It was complicated, but it was also simple. "Because I couldn't be in a relationship with someone actively trying to dismantle everything my family has worked for. I asked him to let it go, but he said no. And that was that."

"He chose money over you?" he asked in surprise. "He'll live to regret that."

Bartholomew didn't seem like the type to have regrets. "My father thinks I might be able to change his mind, but I already asked him once, and he said no."

"Distance makes the heart grow fonder. Maybe he'll miss you enough to give a different answer."

I shook my head. I knew that man. He would never change his mind. "Let's hope so...because we're fucked."

I pulled my knees closer to my chest and circled them with my arms. "Really?"

He nodded. "We're so fucked. He can easily bleed us out until we've got nothing left. We either meet his demands, or he just waits until the money runs out and we're powerless. He can either kill us all then…or just take over. Some of the guys are talking about fleeing to Greece if things don't take a turn."

"What are his demands?"

"No idea. He hasn't made contact."

"Why don't you make contact with him?"

"Because that's what he's expecting. The second he let you go, he knew you would tell us. He's probably waiting to see what we'll do. And once we do, he'll hit us, blow us up, et cetera."

"He's not going to blow you up."

"How do you know?"

"He told me he doesn't intend to kill anyone if they cooperate."

"Cooperate how?"

"He didn't say. And honestly, I didn't want to know."

23

BARTHOLOMEW

I stared out the window of my study for a long time before I finally grabbed the phone. The number was saved into my phone, so I dialed it before I pressed it to my ear. It rang a few times before his arrogant voice answered. "Yes?"

"Leonardo." It was the first time we'd spoken, and without sharing my name, he knew exactly who I was.

He made that clear in his silence. Like a cliché, he thought he had more power by not speaking, but the truth was, he just wasn't man enough to hold his own.

"You're stranded on an island, and no one is coming to your rescue, Leonardo. Either starve to death or accept my terms."

"We can discuss your terms in person. Give me the time and place."

A smile pulled at my lips. "She's not going to change my mind."

"We'll see about that."

Laura was his final weapon. She wanted to protect her family from my wrath, so it wouldn't surprise me if she offered to plead on her father's behalf. She could pitch her case all she wanted, but her beauty wouldn't faze me. Our memories together wouldn't soften my resolve. "Won't make a difference, but perhaps seeing your daughter work against me will teach you to appreciate her. It'll teach you to respect her."

It was three a.m.

The shops and bars were closed, so the Piazza Della Signoria was empty. The replica statue of David stood tall for locals and tourists to admire. The Duomo loomed over us with its height, casting a shadow in the darkness. I'd had several meetings in this square, one of the few places where there was enough space for two militias to meet out in the open.

I sat in the back seat of the SUV and waited, our crew driving off the road to park on the cobblestones. Our fleet of vehicles was bulletproof, and I was certain Leonardo's was as well. An extra car was parked out back, armed with a bazooka if we needed it.

Hopefully, it wouldn't come to that.

Twenty minutes later, headlights appeared. They drove off the road and directly into the plaza, leaving their cars a hundred feet away.

Bleu sat beside me in the car. "How do you want to play this?"

"Leonardo will try to kill me."

He pressed his fingers to his ear as he listened to the guys on the radio. "Our shooters say he has men positioned in some of the windows."

"Take them out." My guys would sneak into the buildings and knock them out cold.

"We'll be ready to take down Leonardo."

"When I deny Laura, it'll be a shootout. The only way to keep his business and his legacy will be to put me in the ground." If I killed her father, Laura and I would truly be done. There would be no going back after that. "Make sure the men get Laura out of there safely."

Bleu gave a nod in confirmation.

The cars stopped, and the headlights went dark.

"Showtime." I stepped out of the car, and that was when the rest of my men followed suit. A flurry of doors opened and closed, and Leonardo and his men mimicked our movements. In my leather jacket and boots, I approached the no-man's-land between us, the statue of David watching on in horror.

Both sides approached the middle, illuminated by the lampposts spaced around the sidewalks. The other statues stared on, stone-faced, watching the late-night throwdown. I walked up to Leonardo and stopped feet away.

Victor and Lucas were there. Lucas kept his vicious eyes focused on me, probably still wearing the gauze underneath his clothes. Other men were stationed there, sporting their assault rifles and handguns.

I kept my eyes glued to Leonardo—but I wanted to search for Laura.

For a man in his fifties, he was in fairly good shape, but his gut was unmistakable. The product of too much wine and liquor. Probably too much bread too. He gave me that stone-cold look, like it might intimidate me.

A stretch of silence ensued, the city quiet. A man left one of the shops and locked the door behind him. When he noticed us, he looked scared shitless because he'd stepped onto the street at the worst possible time. He took off at a dead run.

Leonardo turned and gestured to his men.

Here we go.

The door to one of the SUVs opened and she appeared, dressed in formfitting jeans and boots with a tight sweater that showed off the tits I used to caress with my hands and mouth. When her eyes found mine, there was a hesitation, like a wave of emotions swept over her at the sight of me.

I felt nothing—because I couldn't feel anything right now.

She stopped beside her father, right in front of me. A breeze moved through her hair and ruffled it. The lampposts behind me reflected in her bright eyes. She always appeared confident in her skin, but not tonight. Now she looked like she couldn't string two words together.

It was the first time she'd met me—the *real* me.

Her eyes flicked back and forth between mine, like she was scared of the man who stood before her.

She should be. "Make your plea, sweetheart."

The endearment seemed to pull her back together. "Let this go, Bartholomew."

"No."

"You have France. You have Croatia—"

"And now I want Italy."

"But you don't need it—"

"Don't tell me what I need." I kept my voice low, but she still flinched when I cut her off. "Your father is a fucking asshole who doesn't care about you or anyone else. Despite your estrangement, you would still do anything for him—but he wouldn't do the same for you. I couldn't care less about dismantling his business and his legacy. Regimes rise and fall every day—and now it's his time."

Her eyes hardened when she didn't get the answer she wanted. "Please—"

"No."

"Not even for me? Not even because I'm the one asking?"

I gave a subtle shake of my head. "I wouldn't do it for anyone, sweetheart."

She sucked in a breath like that was a slap in the face. "This isn't going to make you happy, Bartholomew. More money...more power...it's not going to change anything."

"The only people who say those things are poor because they don't know any better."

"Bartholomew—"

"We can continue to waste our time arguing, but it's not going to change anything. Your father will submit to me and become my distributor for a small cut, or he'll be slaughtered in this square along with all the people who are stupid enough to stand by him—except for you. Now get back in the car and drive away, Laura."

She seemed to have finally given up. Now she understood she knew a very different version of me, one that kissed her shoulder when she slept, one that held her close as the morning sun crept across the bed, one that would kill anyone who fucked with her. But that version wasn't here right now. He only existed in the shadows. Only existed behind locked doors.

She stepped back and turned away.

I looked at Leonardo, ready to destroy him.

He moved fast for a man decades older than me. He snatched Laura by the hair and threw her down to the cobblestones. The gun was cocked then pointed at the back of her head.

She screamed so loud that I knew they hadn't rehearsed this.

Laura tried to fight his hold, throwing out her arms then trying to get to her feet. "What the fuck are you doing?"

He smashed the butt of the gun into her head—and then the blood came.

I sucked in a breath through my clenched teeth, traumatized by his brutality.

She turned quiet and slumped over slightly, stunned by the hit.

Leonardo had his eyes locked on me, no remorse whatsoever. "Release the embargo with the distributors in Morocco. Now."

It was the first time in my life I was too stunned to react. My eyes kept glancing to Laura on the ground, the blood darkening in her hair then dripping down onto her sweater.

"Or I'll shoot her."

I knew Leonardo was a motherfucker, but I'd never suspected he was capable of this. "This is how you negotiate?" I asked with a calm voice. "You use your daughter? I've seen a lot of shit…but never this."

He pointed the gun at her arm—and fired.

The sound of the gun echoed through the plaza.

Her screams…were horrific.

Blood immediately soaked her sweater, and she screamed as she grasped her arm, slumped to the ground as she whimpered in pain. Victor tried to break ranks to rush to her aid, but one of the guys put a gun to his head.

Jesus fucking Christ.

"Call off the embargo, or I'll shoot her in the head next time." He continued to grip her hair, his gun pressed right into her first wound.

"Alright!" I wanted to rush to Laura and apply pressure, but I couldn't move, not when Leonardo moved the gun back to her head. "I'll call it off. Let her go."

The asshole had the nerve to grin—fucking grin. "Guess she does mean something to you."

"And nothing to you." I moved to her, but he tugged her back.

"Make the call."

"She'll bleed out—"

"Then you better move quick." He kept the gun pressed to her scalp.

She cried, and I knew it wasn't from the pain in her arm, but her heart.

I pulled out the phone and put the call on speaker. My contact picked up after several rings. "Continue your relationship with Leonardo. Our business has concluded."

He hesitated because this was not the plan we'd established. "Bartholomew, are you sure—"

"When am I not sure about something?" I raised my voice, watching Laura clutch her arm on the ground. "Do as I say. Now."

"Alright."

I hung up and shoved the phone into my pocket, never taking my eyes off Leonardo. "I did as you asked. Now let her go."

"How do I know you aren't going to call when I let her go?"

"Because I give you my fucking word. Now give her to me!"

"You leave my territory and never come back."

"Fine."

He finally pulled the gun from her head. "I'm sorry, Laura. Nothing personal."

I ran to her and gathered her in my arms. She held her arm as she sobbed, angry tears running down her face. She seemed to be in shock because her face was whiter than snow. I lifted her in my arms and turned my back on Leonardo and his men. "I got you, sweetheart."

"He shot me…"

"You'll be alright."

She didn't seem to hear what I said. "My father…shot me."

Then the gunshots started.

I ran to the car, carrying her in my arms, bullets hitting the cars. Their snipers were down and mine took out the other assault rifles. A bullet hit me in the back and made me grunt, but my vest protected me from the worst of it. Then a bullet hit me in the arm. I felt the blood flood the sleeve of my jacket.

I got her into the car, and the driver took off.

I ripped off the sleeve of her sweater and saw her normally olive skin covered in scarlet blood. I grabbed the emergency bandages and secured them around her wound, applying the right pressure to stop the bleeding.

She panted. She cried. Her eyes looked weak, like she was already slipping away.

"Sweetheart, look at me."

After a short fight, she lifted her gaze and looked at me. Her expression changed, falling into despair.

"You're going to be okay. But I need you to stay with me until we get to the hospital. Okay?"

She gave a slight nod.

"Eyes on me."

She gave another nod. "I...I can't believe he did that."

I was an idiot for not anticipating it. A fucking idiot.

"I'm so sorry..." Her eyes dropped, and then she leaned against the seat, suddenly looking very tired. "I'm sorry..."

"Sweetheart, stay with me."

Her eyes closed.

"Stay with me."

I made my choice...and it was the wrong one. Bartholomew is the only man who's ever truly cared about me. He's given me his fidelity, his loyalty, his everything. I hope I can make this right…because I'll die if he walks away. **Read Book Two, Barbarian**, to see if I succeed.

In the meantime, check out Hartrow's brand-new author Tamara Balliana. She's written an incredible romantic comedy that readers will love.

Penelope Sky would like to give a personal introduction.

> I rarely read romantic comedies, but this book was so great that it stayed with me long after I finished it. It's one of those feel-good, funny, endearing stories where you just get attached to the characters. You've got Finn, this stubborn, hard-headed cop (who the heroine describes as having a stick up his ass LMAO) and of course, he's HAWT. Roxane happened to be in the wrong place at the wrong time, witnessing a murder, and now that murderer wants her head too. Turns out, the only person that can protect her is this sexy, brooding cop that's been obsessed

with catching this guy for years. When these two characters are together, the chemistry is off the pages. The banter, oh my lord, is hilarious. Watching these two argumentative and confrontational characters soften for one another was deeply satisfying. Hartwick asked me to read just the first book, but I liked it so much, I've read them all. Each book is a standalone, but the next books are about Finn's brothers...who are also HAWT. Cops, firefighters, lawyers...all tough guys that turn to goddamn mush when the right woman walks in. 5 Stars. No, I take that back. 10 stars. Ms. Balliana earned it.

Check out reviews from our other authors:

"Sooooo good. Funny. Sexy. Endearing. It has all the elements I love in a romance. I love romantic comedies, and this is a story that belongs on Netflix or the big screen. There's this scene with a vindictive chicken when they're cooped up in the country house...you'll have to read it to see what I mean. But it's hilarious. Totally 5 Stars."

E. L. Todd

New York Times bestselling author

"I read books in all kinds of genres. A good story is a good story, regardless of the label it gets. Well, this is a fantastic romantic comedy. Not only is it funny, but it's heartwarming, sexy, and just plain fun. I flipped through the pages of this standalone like a mad woman, and then I immediately asked for the other books in the series because these Rossi brothers are HAWT. Cops, firefighters, and lawyers...they're so sexy. And the women are hot too. I could see myself getting a drink with all of them and having a night on the town."

Victoria Quinn

New York Times bestselling author

Order Now or Read in KU!

Printed in Great Britain
by Amazon